He'd Been Thinking Of Her In Ways He Shouldn't Have Been.

Her laughter echoed in his head; her face filled his mind. His hands itched to cup her breasts, mold her hips. He couldn't remember when a woman had gotten under his skin the way Jessica had. Being with her every day was working on him, and seeing her in that wet gown only added fuel to the fire smoldering inside.

Man, get a grip, he told himself. *She's off-limits.*

He strode outside to the pool, stripped and dived in.

No matter how fast he swam, he couldn't escape the thoughts of her, the bone-deep aching that bedeviled him. He was asking for trouble, keeping Jessica around, but he couldn't turn her out when she needed help. He owed it to the brother he never knew.

Somehow he would manage to keep his hands in his pockets and his thoughts to himself.

Somehow.

Dear Reader,

Welcome to Silhouette Desire, where you can spice up your April with six passionate, powerful and provocative romances!

Beloved author Diana Palmer delivers a great read with *A Man of Means,* the latest in her LONG, TALL TEXANS miniseries, as a saucy cook tames a hot-tempered cowboy with her biscuits. Then, enjoy reading how one woman's orderly life is turned upside down when she is wooed by *Mr. Temptation,* April's MAN OF THE MONTH and the first title in Cait London's hot new HEARTBREAKERS miniseries.

Reader favorite Maureen Child proves a naval hero is no match for a determined single mom in *The SEAL's Surrender,* the latest DYNASTIES: THE CONNELLYS title. And a reluctant widow gets a second chance at love in *Her Texan Tycoon* by Jan Hudson.

The drama continues in the TEXAS CATTLEMAN'S CLUB: THE LAST BACHELOR continuity series with *Tall, Dark...and Framed?* by Cathleen Galitz, when an attractive defense attorney falls head over heels for her client—a devastatingly handsome tycoon with a secret. And discover what a ranch foreman, a virgin and her protective brothers have in common in *One Wedding Night...* by Shirley Rogers.

Celebrate the season by pampering yourself with all six of these exciting new love stories.

Enjoy!

Joan Marlow Golan

Joan Marlow Golan
Senior Editor, Silhouette Desire

Please address questions and book requests to:
Silhouette Reader Service
U.S.: 3010 Walden Ave., P.O. Box 1325, Buffalo, NY 14269
Canadian: P.O. Box 609, Fort Erie, Ont. L2A 5X3

Her Texan Tycoon
JAN HUDSON

Published by Silhouette Books
America's Publisher of Contemporary Romance

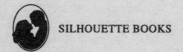 SILHOUETTE BOOKS

ISBN 0-373-76432-4

HER TEXAN TYCOON

Visit Silhouette at www.eHarlequin.com

Printed in U.S.A.

Books by Jan Hudson

Silhouette Desire

In Roared Flint #1035
One Ticket to Texas #1071
Plain Jane's Texan #1229
Wild About a Texan #1425
Her Texan Tycoon #1432

JAN HUDSON,

a winner of the Romance Writers of America RITA®
Award, is a native Texan who lives with her husband in
historically rich Nacogdoches, the oldest town in Texas.
Formerly a licensed psychologist, she taught college
psychology for over a decade before becoming a full-
time author. Jan loves to write fast-paced stories laced
with humor, fantasy and adventure, and with bold char-
acters who reach beyond the mundane and celebrate life.

Special thanks to Terrie Crockett
of Crockett Farms in Harlingen for her help
in educating me about the citrus business in the
Texas Valley and for the tour of the groves.

Thanks also to the nice folks
at the Harlingen, Texas, Chamber of Commerce
and Visitors' Center for their assistance.

One

Smith Rutledge glanced up from his macaroni and cheese to spot a young woman in khaki shorts, an oversize shirt and a bucket hat. She was holding her food tray and looking around for an empty table in the crowded Harlingen, Texas, cafeteria.

Nice legs had been his first thought, his interest aroused. He was admiring the rest of the package when her scan of the room stopped on him.

Their gazes met, locked, and he was halfway to his feet to offer her a place at his table when her eyes widened and a horrified expression blanched her face.

"Tom!" she cried. Her eyes rolled back, and both she and the tray crashed to the floor.

On her heels was a hulking biker with tattoos on

both beefy forearms. He slipped and slammed down on top of her, his overladen tray hitting her as well.

The noisy room went suddenly quiet. Everybody but Smith seemed to be in suspended animation. He jumped to his feet and ran to help the woman.

The biker, covered in mashed potatoes, gravy and cherry cobbler, found his legs. "Man, what happened?" the burly guy asked.

"I think she fainted," Smith told him. "Get the manager." He squatted beside the fallen woman and checked for a pulse. Strong beat, thank God, but she was out cold and a cut on her forehead was bleeding profusely.

The manager came rushing up. "I've called 911. An ambulance is on the way. What happened, Mr. Rutledge?"

"I don't know, Juan. She just suddenly keeled over, and the guy behind her fell on top of her. She's unconscious."

Smith didn't add that she'd fainted after seeing him, that she'd looked at him as if he were Hannibal Lecter. Hell, he might not be as pretty as his brother Kyle or his lady-killer Crow cousins, but he usually didn't have that kind of effect on women. And who the devil was Tom?

The EMT crew came rushing in with a stretcher and a medical kit—and a slew of questions he couldn't answer. He didn't know her name, much less if she was diabetic or had any allergies.

Smith picked up her purse, a denim sack that felt as if she carried a bowling ball in it, and hunted for a wallet with some identification. He found a red leather one, and when he opened it, he froze.

There, smiling up from a plastic pocket, was a picture of him. How did she get a picture of him? He'd never seen the woman in his life. He flipped to the next photo, and there was a picture of them together. What the—

"Sir, sir," the tech said. "We need to take her to the emergency room. What's her name?"

Dazed, Smith stared at him, trying to register the question.

"Her name?"

He quickly glanced at the driver's license. "Jessica O'Connor Smith. Her name is Jessica O'Connor Smith. I'm coming with you."

"Sir, you can't ride in the ambulance."

"Then I'll be right behind you." Smith stuck the wallet in his coat pocket, and, still carrying her denim bag, hurried after the stretcher.

Smith sat in one of the plastic chairs in the waiting room, then rose and paced. He'd been alternately sitting and pacing outside the emergency room for the past hour. He'd tried to go into the room with the woman, but a broad-shouldered nurse, who wasn't swayed by the amount of money Smith had contributed to the hospital, had ordered him out.

"You'll just be in the way," the nurse had told him. "The doctor will speak to you when he's done."

"He's taking his own sweet time," Smith muttered to no one in particular. He was concerned about the woman, sure, but he was more concerned about what he'd found in her wallet.

He sat down and looked at the photographs again. He must have stared at those two pictures a dozen times while he waited, trying to figure out where and when they were taken. For the life of him, he couldn't remember.

Once, years ago, he'd drunk too much tequila with some of his college buddies and woke up two days later, pockets empty and confused, in a seedy Matamoros hotel. Scared the dickens out of him, too. But that had only happened once. He'd learned his lesson. Except for an occasional glass of wine or bottle of beer, he didn't drink.

Frowning, he studied the picture of Jessica O'Connor Smith and him. Pretty woman, dynamite smile. He wouldn't have forgotten somebody like her. Her blondish hair was shorter and sleeker in the photo. Now it was long and curly, and she wore it in a single thick braid, but it was definitely the same woman.

Jessica O'Connor Smith of 218 Elm Street, Bartlesville, Oklahoma, her driver's license said. Smith didn't think he'd ever even passed through Bartlesville. He'd also found a library card, a voter registration, a single credit card and twenty-eight dollars in cash in her wallet. Her bag was filled with more junk than he could have imagined toting around with him, but there was nothing more that told him anything about her. No address book, no personal letters. He'd searched the purse thoroughly.

The O'Connor sounded like a last name, too. Was

it her maiden name? Was she married? She wasn't wearing a wedding ring. He'd noted that early on. There wasn't even a telltale tan line where one might have been.

She was probably a tourist, one of the countless visitors that fled the colder parts of the country to bask in the sunshine of the Texas Rio Grande Valley's early spring. Lots of folks, especially older ones, wintered over in the Valley, but she certainly wasn't a senior citizen.

He'd even tried calling Bartlesville information, thinking to locate her family, but the operator informed him that there were no Smiths listed at the address he'd given her. Odd. But maybe she had an unlisted number there.

"Mr. Smith?"

Smith glanced up to see a doctor. He stood. "No, I'm Smith Rutledge."

"Sorry. I must have been confused. I thought the patient's last name was Smith. Are you her husband?"

"Her last name *is* Smith, and I'm not her husband. Just...an acquaintance."

"Ah, of course. You're Smith Rutledge of Smith Corp, the computer company. Sorry I didn't recognize you at first, Mr. Rutledge," the doctor said. He was obviously more impressed with Smith's hospital donations than the nurse.

"How is Ms. Smith doing?"

"Dazed, confused. The cut on her forehead isn't serious. I've closed it with a butterfly, but she may have a concussion, and she injured her wrist. We're waiting for a report from X-ray now. From what Ms. Smith told me, I gather that she'd skipped a couple of meals. I suspect her blood sugar dropped, and she fainted. We're doing tests, but I'm sure that she's going to be fine.''

"She's awake then? May I see her?''

"Not just yet, Mr. Rutledge. The nurse will keep you posted. Would you like some coffee while you wait?''

Smith shook his head and took up pacing again.

Another hour passed before the nurse appeared. "We're having problems with Ms. Smith. The doctor's orders call for her to stay overnight, but she insists on leaving. Wants her RV, she says. Says she doesn't have insurance and can't afford to pay for what we've done already. Mr. Rutledge, she shouldn't leave. She's groggy from pain meds and has an IV going and a cast on her arm. She can't drive, for goodness' sakes. Can you do something with her?''

Smith stood. "I can try.''

The woman he found in the room was a far cry from the one in the photograph—and from the agitated one the nurse described. This one had a bandage on her forehead, a cast on her arm from knuckles to elbow, and the IV was intact. Her face pale against the white pillow, her eyelids brushed with haggard blue, she was sleeping like a baby. Something about her total vulnerability as she lay on that sterile gurney struck a responsive chord in him. He felt a powerful protective streak stir inside his chest, and when he heard what was going on, fury flashed over him.

Another woman with a clipboard stood beside the bed shaking her. "Ms. Smith, Ms. Smith, I need to know the name of your insurance company. What is your address? Who is your next of kin? Ms. Smith?"

"Leave her alone," Smith said sharply.

"But I have to find out who's responsible for her bill, sir."

"I am." He took a business card from his pocket and thrust it at her. "Send her bill to my office. Now get out of here."

The woman stiffened and clutched her clipboard to her ample bosom. "Sir, I'm just doing my job."

Smith raked his hand over his face. "Of course. Excuse us, please."

He stood there and stared down at the sleeping woman for the longest time, fighting his own impulse to shake her awake. He had plenty of questions of his own. But now wasn't the time to ask them.

"I guess the Demerol finally kicked in," the nurse said. "We'll be moving her to a private room in a few minutes."

"Put her in a suite," Smith said.

"But, sir, I don't have the authority to—"

Smith handed another of his business cards to the nurse. "Call the hospital administrator, please. Tell him that I would like to speak with him immediately."

If Jessica Smith was staying overnight, so was he. He wasn't about to let her out of his sight until he had some answers.

Shortly after Smith spoke with the administrator, Jessica was moved to a well-appointed suite reserved for VIPs. She slept through the entire process.

Hoping that she would awaken soon and he could ask about the photographs, Smith sat in a recliner next to her bed, watching and waiting.

She slept on.

By midnight, he was familiar with every attribute of her face, down to the tiny freckle just beneath her left eyebrow. She was an attractive woman with strong features: high cheekbones, full lips and a hint of a cleft in her chin—though hers was not nearly as deep as his.

Once, when she'd grown restless, he'd stroked wispy ringlets away from her temples, held her hand and murmured soothing sounds. It had seemed the most natural thing in the world for him to do. Her right hand, the uninjured one, still grasped his thumb like a lifeline.

Her nails were short and shaped, with no polish on them. He checked again for rings. She wore none. In fact, she wore no jewelry of any kind—though he did notice that her ears were pierced—two holes in each lobe. The nurse had given him Jessica's watch to keep. It was a cheap brand available from most discount stores.

Earlier, he'd even searched the clothes she'd been wearing, hoping something in her pockets might reveal more information. All he'd found was half a roll of antacids and seventy-two cents in change. He did discover that the designer-brand shorts were size eight, the white tank top a medium, and her cotton bra was a 34C. He was polite enough not to examine her panties closely, except to note that they were plain and utilitarian. Her well-worn white sneakers were size seven.

The shirt, a frayed blue chambray, was a sixteen and a half/thirty-six—more his size than hers. Smith wondered about the man who'd been the shirt's original owner, but there were no laundry markings to give him a clue.

About two-thirty in the morning, Jessica grew restless, and she thrashed about and whimpered in her sleep. The sound cut him to the quick.

"Shh," he whispered, stroking back the damp ringlets. "Rest easy."

Her eyes fluttered open, and when she saw him, she smiled. "Tom, you're here," she said, her words slurred. "You must be an angel."

She squeezed his hand and fell back asleep.

Two

Her head hurt. And she'd had the strangest dream. Squinting against the sunlight flooding her room, Jessica forced open her eyes and looked around. Everything seemed so white. She felt confused as she tried to figure out where she was.

Her arm hurt, and something heavy held down her leg. She managed to lift her head and saw that her hand and arm were in a cast. A man's head rested against her leg, and she immediately recognized the shock of wiry auburn hair.

Jessica's heart leapt to her throat. "Tom!" she gasped.

But it *couldn't* be Tom. Tom was *dead.* He'd died two years ago.

Yet, when the head jerked up, Tom's hazel eyes

looked at her. Eyes more green than hazel really. Eyes so expressive that they telegraphed his every mood. They were strong and clear instead of filled with pain, and his body was sturdy and healthy again instead of— *Oh, Lord!*

"Did I die?" she asked. "Is this heaven?"

"Die? Heaven?" He scowled. "What are you talking about? You're in the hospital. In Harlingen, Texas. You were hurt. Don't you remember?"

Jessica rubbed her head and blinked her eyes several times, trying to shake the dream. Tom didn't disappear. Her heart began to race, and alarm burgeoned inside her. "Wh—why are you here?"

"I'm here for some answers. Just who the devil *are* you?"

"I'm Jessica, your wife. Don't you recognize me?"

"Lady, until I saw you in the cafeteria last night, I'd never laid eyes on you in my life. What's your game?"

Her heart pounded faster, and her mouth went bone-dry. "I don't know what you're talking about." She struggled to sit up, meaning to bolt, but things went woozy, and Tom grabbed her.

"Take it easy. You have an IV in your arm, and you need to stay in bed."

The hands on her shoulders felt very warm and very real. She could even smell the aftershave he always wore. Panic gripped her chest and her heart was in her throat. "You're frightening me. Go away, Tom. Just go away. You're *dead.*"

She squeezed her eyes shut and prayed.

"I'm not dead. Here, feel." He took her hand and stamped it over his face. "I'm very much alive. And my name isn't Tom."

Her eyes popped open, and she stared at the man. Her fingers moved over the familiar nose, the deep cleft in his chin. "You look like Tom. You feel like Tom. You sound like Tom. I don't understand what's happening. Who are you?"

"I'm Smith Rutledge. Smith Allan Rutledge. Chairman of the board of Smith Corp, the computer manufacturing company. Ring any bells?"

She shook her head. "Not really. Except…I have a blue Smith laptop. *That* Smith?"

"That's the one. Now, who are you? And who is this Tom you've been talking about?"

"I'm Jessica O'Connor *Smith*. And Tom, Thomas Edward *Smith*, is—*was* my husband. You look exactly—"

A white-coated man and a nurse breezed in the door. "Good morning, Jessica," the man said. "I'm Dr. Vargas. How are you feeling this morning? Better?"

"I'm feeling fine, thank you. I need to get out of here. I don't have any insurance. I can't afford this," she said, gesturing over the room with her good arm. "The bill must be astronomical."

Dr. Vargas smiled. "Don't worry about the bill. Just concentrate on recovery. I've looked over all your tests, and, except for your being anemic, everything checks out okay. You can go home. I'll give you a diet and a prescription for medication for the anemia as well as some pain pills for your wrist."

She lifted her casted hand. "What happened?"

"You fractured your wrist. It will be as good as new in about six weeks. You can come back and see me then unless you have a problem. We can recheck your hemoglobin then, too."

"*Six weeks?* But I don't even live here. I'm on my way to Brownsville, well, Matamoros really. I planned to leave the RV in Brownsville and have a—" Jessica stopped abruptly, realizing that she was babbling. "Sorry," she said.

"You're driving an RV?" the doctor asked as he tore the prescriptions from his pad. "Alone?"

"Yes, of course."

"I wouldn't recommend driving for a while, especially not an RV. And with the anemia, I'd like you to rest and follow this regimen until we see if it clears up. If not, we'll need to do some further tests."

"But I can't stay here, Dr. Vargas. I don't know anyone here, and besides, I have work to do, and—"

Smith Rutledge deftly slipped the papers from the doctor's hand. "I'll see that she follows orders, Dr. Vargas."

"Ah, very good, Mr. Rutledge. We at Valley Memorial are always happy to be of service." He patted Jessica's knee, smiled broadly and said, "I'll see you in six weeks." With that, he whirled and was out the door.

"Just what do you mean that *you'll* see that I follow orders? Who do you think you are?"

For the first time he grinned, although his expression had a definite menacing air. "I thought we had already established that. I'm Smith Rutledge, the man who wants some answers, and I'm taking you home with me."

"Like hell you are!"

Jessica was never quite sure how he pulled it off. Even with the hospital administrator and the chief of staff vouching for the sterling character of one of the town's leading citizens, she had no intention of letting him take her anywhere. Maybe the drugs made her too goofy to be sensible, or maybe it was simply befuddlement over the man who was a dead ringer for Tom that overcame her defenses. In any case, she found herself swaddled in a blanket in the front seat of Smith Rutledge's very fancy SUV, a pillow under her arm and her belongings in a plastic bag in the back seat.

"I'm really concerned about my RV," she said. "Almost everything I own is in it, and it's still parked in the lot at the cafeteria."

"Not a problem. One of my men is moving it to the farm. In fact, it ought to be there by the time we are."

Stunned, she stared at him. "Where did you get the keys?"

"From that monster of a purse you had with you."

"You looked in my purse?"

"Of course I did. How else could I have gotten your name? You were out cold."

She started to protest, then sighed and rubbed her head.

"Head hurting?" he asked.

"A little. I'm very sensitive to painkillers. My

brain is foggy, and I have a humongous hangover. Plus, this whole thing is bizarre. I feel as if I'm in the middle of a dream. It's uncanny how much you look like my husband. I've heard that everybody has a double somewhere in the world, but I'd never believed it before. It's weird. And what a coincidence that we met."

"I don't believe in coincidences," he said tersely. "And that business about doubles is garbage."

Dumbfounded by his comments, she could only stare at him for a moment. "Then how else can you explain it? You look exactly like Tom."

"I can't explain it, but I mean for you to."

He turned onto a road bounded by rows and rows of small trees and waved to a guard at the gate. They passed under a huge arched sign that said Sugartime Farms. At least that's what she thought it said. She'd had to squint to read the letters, and they'd been wavy.

"How can I explain what I don't understand?" she asked.

"We'll talk later. We're almost there."

"Almost where?"

"My house."

She glanced around at the groves they drove through. "Yours?"

He nodded.

"What kind?"

"Grapefruit and orange."

"That's a lot of juice."

He nodded again. "I have about two thousand acres in groves."

"I'm allergic to grapefruit."

"Does being around trees bother you?"

"I don't think so. Just eating the pulp or drinking the juice. My lips swell, and I break out in hives. Odd, but I'm not allergic to oranges or lemons or limes. Just grapefruit." She sighed and leaned her head against the side window.

"Sorry about that. Our Ruby Reds are some of the finest in the Valley."

He turned into a circular driveway and stopped in front of a house that astonished her. The huge Spanish-style place with its tiled roof and stuccoed walls looked like something she might have pictured in Beverly Hills. Bougainvillea and other lush plants spilled from urns and hanging baskets that were everywhere, and she counted three elaborate fountains ringed with more flowers.

She tried not to act like an awestruck kid, but even in her muzzy state she was indeed awestruck. "Your place is magnificent."

"Thanks. I like it."

She was still gawking when he came around and helped her from the vehicle. Moving hurt, but she tried not to wince.

He frowned. "You need another pain pill. I hope the nurse is here."

"What nurse?"

"The nurse that's coming to take care of you."

"Aw, jeez! Another pain pill is the last thing I need. And I don't need a nurse. It's only a banged-up wrist." She held up the arm in cast and sling.

"And anemia. The doctor said you need special care for that."

"What special care? A couple of iron pills a day and an extra helping of liver and onions ought to do it. It's no big deal."

"It *is* a big deal. I agreed to supervise your recuperation, and I intend to do it, Jessica. Let's get you set up in your room. You can rest a while, then we'll talk."

He started to steer her forward, but she balked and dug in her heels. "Hold it, mister. Did anybody ever tell you that you're like a steamroller?"

A hint of a smile played at one corner of his mouth. "Not lately."

"Too scared of the boss, huh? Well, let me tell you, you're like a steamroller, and I don't like it. You may be the head honcho of a big corporation and of all this—" she waved her good hand "—but you're not my boss, so back off. I don't even know why I agreed to come with you anyhow. This was a bad idea."

His eyebrows shot up. "Was it? I wonder."

His words dripped with hidden meaning, but she was too foggy to spar with him. All she could think of was lying down and sleeping for four or five days. She stumbled.

He grabbed her elbow. "Easy."

A tall woman in white hurried out. "Hi, I'm Kathy McCauley, the R.N. from the service. Let me help."

"I'm fine," Jessica insisted. "It's just the Demerol. It knocked me on my butt. I need to lie down."

She stumbled again, and Smith caught her. He

swung her up into his arms and carried her toward the door.

"Let me down. I'm too heavy. I can walk."

"Shh," he said. "Stop wiggling. You're light as a feather."

"I'm not light."

"I lift weights. Trust me. You're light."

Her wiggling stopped, and she relaxed against him, her arm around his neck, her head on his shoulder. It seemed like the most natural thing in the world. She felt safe. For the first time in ages, she felt safe.

After Jessica was installed in a guest suite near his own rooms and the nurse had reported that she was asleep, Smith headed for the barn. The RV, a smallish older model that had seen better days, was parked beside the building. Since Smith had been the target of scams before, he considered calling his security chief but decided against it. He could handle this himself.

He hesitated only a moment before opening the door and climbing inside. He meant to search every inch of the place and come up with some answers.

After an hour, all he came up with was more questions. In a beat-up chest, he found three pair of jeans, two pair of shorts, two sweatshirts, sweatpants, and six T-shirts and assorted tops along with more plain underwear. All of the clothing was inexpensive and well worn, except for one pair of designer jeans. Hanging in a small closet were a long black leather coat and a blue down jacket. Also hanging there, in cleaner bags, were two suits, a pair of slacks, a dress, three silk blouses and a cotton sweater set. He didn't know much about women's clothes, but he could tell from the fabric and the tailoring that they were expensive. When he tried to check the labels, he discovered that they had been clipped off. Odd.

Besides two nice-looking pair of high heels, well-shined loafers and a fancy pair of boots, she had the usual stash of women's stuff. He rummaged through lotions and makeup and such, noting that most of hers was of the drugstore variety except for some samples of what appeared to be more expensive lines, including several tiny vials of perfume—must have been twenty or thirty of them, all different.

Her towels were frayed, and her toothbrush was about worn out. An oversize T-shirt and a tattered bathrobe hung on a hook in the bathroom. The only jewelry he located were two pair of small hoops, one gold, one silver, and a silver butterfly pin.

Her food stash consisted of cereal, peanut butter, bread, crackers and soup. Lots of soup. There were both cans and packets of the dried variety, mostly chicken noodle and vegetable. Hell, if this is what she ate, no wonder she was anemic.

Her bunk was neatly made with a quilt, and her pillow had a blue satin case. A big stuffed monkey lay beside her pillow. It was the ugliest damn monkey he'd ever seen in his life. Taped underneath an overhead cabinet so that they were visible from the bed were several index cards with motivational slogans and other gung-ho sayings written on them. He smiled as he read, "A quitter never wins" and

"What the mind can conceive, it can achieve." A Cherokee proverb, "Have a vision not clouded by fear" was highlighted in yellow.

In a cabinet under the bunk, he found a stack of paperback books, a flashlight, a sewing machine in a latched case and another case full of all kinds of thread and needles and pins. When he opened the lid of a bench seat, he discovered a locked briefcase. Also inside were the blue Smith laptop she'd mentioned and a small printer, both last year's model. He'd take the computer and the briefcase into the house and examine them later.

The rest of the area was crammed with boxes.

He went through every blasted one of them.

Most of them were full of purses. He'd never seen so many purses outside a department store. The biggest part of them were like that muncher she carried, some denim, some black, some tan. They were all the same style, half backpack/half purse, with a wide adjustable shoulder strap and a bunch of zippered pockets on the outside. Other boxes were filled with dainty little purses, some beaded, some with flowers and tassels or other froufrou. Except for about three basic shapes, no two of them were alike. Other boxes contained what looked like the raw materials for the little purses, all divided and labeled—things like: blue beaded tops, black silk braid, red poppies. There were dozens of boxes of that kind of material as well as boxes filled with boxes.

Smith took out one of the small, custom-made boxes to examine it. Oval-shaped and cream-colored, it had a gold rope handle and was just about the right size to hold one of those little purses. Inside every box were two sheets of cream-colored tissue paper flecked with gold. On the lid of each box, Jessica Miles was written in fancy gold script.

Who the hell was Jessica Miles?

She'd either heisted this stuff or she was selling it.

Then he opened a last box. Office supplies.

Besides several reams of paper, he found brochures, order forms and business cards. All advertised Handbags by Jessica Miles, along with an Oklahoma mailing address, an 800 number and a Web site. He took one of each, stuck them in his pocket, then restacked and secured the boxes—except for one that was almost empty. He dumped the purses from it on her bunk and packed some of her casual clothes and other belongings in it. The rest he would get later.

On his way out, he grabbed the laptop and the briefcase. By the time Sleeping Beauty woke up, he was going to know all about her.

Three

Jessica's eyes popped open. Instantly, she was wide awake and alert. Trouble was, she didn't recognize her surroundings. The room was dim and nothing seemed familiar. The moment she threw back the covers and started out of bed, her injured wrist reminded her. That and the hospital gown she still wore.

It all came back. Smith Rutledge. The man who looked so much like Tom. And whose first name was Smith instead of his last. Odd.

She switched on a lamp, glancing at the clock radio as she did. Six-twelve, the red numbers said. Morning or evening? Rubbing her face, she looked around, taking in the unique Spanish-style furnishings of the room. The walls were pale cream and the floors were terra-cotta tile with a scattering of thick rugs. The soft yellow headboard and the chests were beautifully carved wood with a large calla lily design in bold relief and painted green and white. This was the work of an artisan, she thought as she ran her fingers over the spray of lilies on the bedside table. Magnificent.

A door opened, and the nurse appeared.

"Ah, you're awake," she said. "I was about to rouse you. Mr. Rutledge was concerned that you might miss another meal."

"Another meal?"

"You slept through lunch. It's dinnertime. Mr. Rutledge thought you might like to eat on the patio just outside." The nurse motioned toward draperies across the room. "Feel like it?"

"I think so," Jessica said. "I must have finally slept off the effects of the medication. I never take anything stronger than an aspirin because it simply knocks me for a loop. I barely remember meeting you and going to bed here. And I'm sorry, but I don't remember your name."

The nurse smiled. "You were pretty groggy. I'm Kathy McCauley. Want to wash up a bit?"

"I'd love to, thanks." Her knees were wobbly at first, but Kathy walked her to the bathroom and helped her bathe her face and brush her teeth with a new toothbrush that was laid out on the counter near a collection of pricey lotions and bath products. Jessica noticed that her own makeup bag and hairbrush were there as well.

"Rosa brought some of your things in from your

RV,'' Kathy said. ''Rosa is the housekeeper and a real sweetheart. Want me to help you brush your hair and rebraid it?''

''Please. Looks like doing things with a cast will be tricky until I get the hang of it.'' She sat down on a padded vanity chair while Kathy carefully brushed the tangles from her hair.

''Oh, you'll soon be managing it.'' Kathy, a tallish woman with a sturdy shape and a square face, chattered pleasantly as she worked, then said, ''There, how does that look?''

Jessica held the mirror to admire the very fine French braid. ''Great. Much better than when I do it. You should be a hairdresser.''

Kathy laughed. ''I am. I have three daughters. Let me get a fresh gown and a robe for you to put on. By the way, while you were sleeping, I went to the mall and picked up a couple of gowns and robes with loose sleeves that will be easy for you to wear with your cast. I bought some house slippers and a few other items for you as well.''

Jessica went stone still as the nurse bustled from the room. When she came back with an exquisite blue gown and a matching robe with a zip front, she felt a little sick. ''Kathy, I can't afford those. They look as if they cost a small fortune. I'll have to make do with a T-shirt and sweatpants.''

''You don't have to pay me back. Mr. Rutledge had me charge the whole thing to him. Honey, you're one lucky lady to have a guy like him crazy about you. Not only is he a hunk, he's the richest man in the Valley. The little dab of stuff I bought for you didn't make a dent in his bank account, trust me on that.''

"Crazy about me? What are you talking about?"

Kathy winked. "Don't try to fool me. I recognize all the signs. Why, the man sat beside your bed the whole time I was gone, and he's just about paced a rut outside your door most of the afternoon." She held out the gown. "Slip this on."

The silky fabric felt like heaven against her skin. And the long robe with its kimono sleeves and mandarin collar made her look and feel very elegant, even with the cast and sling. Kathy insisted on her adding a touch of blush and lipstick.

"There, with a little more color, you look fabulous. Ready for dinner?"

"More than ready. I'm suddenly starving. Are you joining me?"

Kathy grinned. "Not on your life. I'm leaving you two alone." She shepherded Jessica across the room and drew the draperies.

A table, complete with flowers and candles, was set on the veranda outside her room.

Smith Rutledge sat in one of the large, cushioned chairs, his feet crossed and his boot heel resting atop a railing. The sight of him startled her anew. It was eerie. A thousand times before the accident, she'd seen Tom sit with his feet propped up like that. She used to fuss at him about scarring his boots, but Tom's boots were never as expensive as the ones Smith wore.

The sound of the doors opening brought Smith to

his feet. He looked her up and down, then smiled. "You look very nice."

She touched her braid, then glanced over her shoulder to Kathy. But Kathy was gone. "Thank you. Thank you very much. I don't know when I'll be able to repay you for all this. It may take a while. My business is—"

"Having a bit of a cash-flow problem?"

"Yes. We're just getting started."

"We?"

"My partner and I. Shirley Miles."

"Ah," he said. "Thus, Handbags by Jessica Miles. You combined the names."

"Yes. How did you know about Jessica Miles?"

"I, er, found a brochure when I was getting some of your things from the RV."

"I thought Rosa got my stuff."

He held her chair as she was seated. "I got your stuff. Rosa put it away in your room."

The thought of him going through her things made her very uncomfortable. She almost said something snippy. Instead, she grabbed the glass of orange juice beside her plate and took a big swig. "Say, this is very good." She drained her glass.

"Thanks. That's from our new Valencia crop."

"You grew the oranges for this juice?"

"Yep. An hour ago, the oranges were still on the tree. We grow both navels and Valencias here. The navels mature earlier and bear through the first of the year. Valencias come on in early February and last until about April or May, so we'll have fresh ones for another two or three months. It's a shame that you can't eat grapefruit. The few Ruby Reds still left on the trees are sweet as honey.

"I checked with a nutritionist and orange juice is supposed to help assimilate iron from food—and the fresher, the better." He picked up a plate and piled on a huge portion of spinach salad from a serving cart near the table. "Spinach is rich in iron," he said as he placed the heaping salad in front of her. He fixed a smaller plate for himself and sat down across from her.

"If I eat all that, you'll be able to pick me up with a magnet."

He grinned. "Did I overdo it?"

"Just a tad."

"Eat what you want and leave the rest. Ric will be here with the entrée in a few minutes."

Eating with her right hand was difficult. And trying to manage food with him staring at her was darned near impossible. When she dropped a forkful for the second time, she said, "Sorry, but this is hard to get used to. I'm a southpaw."

"Don't worry about it. I think you're doing great. Tell me about your business. How did you get started?"

"It's something Shirley and I had talked about for a long time. She and I have been friends since the fourth grade, and we taught at the same school. We were both anxious to make more money than we could earn teaching, so our own business sounded like a good idea. Since I'd been designing and making my own for a long time, the handbags were a natural."

"You're a teacher?"

"Uh-huh. Or was. Junior-high art. I'm on a leave of absence for a year, trying to make a go of the business. Shirley's still teaching math. Since she has a husband and two kids, it was harder for her to take a leave. She runs things at home, and I hit the road."

"Doing what?"

"Finding markets for our handbags, mostly through boutiques, and sometimes making direct sales at various festivals and shows. Our ergonomic Back Buddy is our casual line, and—"

"Your *what?*"

Jessica smiled. "Our ergonomic bag? Well, it's an idea Shirley and I came up with after she hurt her back. There are several similar designs around, but we think ours works best—and it's a lot cheaper than other versions. Mack, Shirley's husband, has an upholstery shop, and his crew makes the bags at off times. Basically, the shoulder bag is designed so that weight is distributed in such a way that a very heavy bag feels much lighter than it is, and it doesn't put as much strain on the shoulder and back."

"Interesting idea. You'll have to show me how it works."

"I'd love to. I have the spiel down pretty pat by now." She smiled brightly. "These bags are fabulous. Women are going wild over them, and your wife or girlfriend will love having one. I can even embroider her name or initials on it to personalize your gift. Would you prefer denim, black or beige, sir? Or perhaps one of each?"

"I don't have a wife or a girlfriend."

"Good-looking guy like you? I don't believe it."

"Believe it."

Keeping in character with her sales patter, she turned up her smile and said, "Then how about your secretary or the women in your office? These bags make wonderful Christmas gifts, and they're very affordable."

Smith chuckled and held up his hands. "You've sold me. I'll take a dozen."

She laughed. "Don't I wish sales were so easy." She turned her attention back to her salad.

"Business not going well?"

She shrugged. "Actually, it's not bad, just hard building our clientele, especially for our upscale evening bags. That's where we hope to make our money. They're one-of-a-kind designer creations that will be carried by the more exclusive boutiques. We've reserved a booth at the Dallas market in mid-April. I've been trying to work on inventory for that show in every spare moment I have.

"I don't know how I'm going to manage it with this." She held up her cast and swallowed back the lump that suddenly formed in her throat. "We've booked a booth at a festival in Corpus Christi next weekend and at an arts and crafts fair in Houston the week after that. And between now and then, I have to locate a woman in Matamoros."

A young man appeared with a tray. "Your dinner, *señor*."

"Thanks, Ric. Have you finished with your salad?" he asked Jessica.

She nodded, surprised to see most of it gone. She must have eaten it all while she was talking.

Ric served their food and left. Liver and onions, potatoes, broccoli. Very large helpings.

"Iron rich?" she asked.

"According to the nutritionist, very."

Jessica hated liver, and she was only moderately tolerant of broccoli, but she didn't want to insult her host. She attacked the liver, heaping onions on each bite and burying it in a blob of potatoes.

"I really appreciate all the trouble you've gone to, particularly since I'm a stranger," she said. "Now that I have my wits back, I'll try to get out of your hair by tomorrow."

"The doctor said you shouldn't be driving. I don't think you can manage an RV with that arm."

"I can hole up in a local RV park, or maybe, after I talk with the woman I'm looking for, I can hire somebody to drive me back to Oklahoma. I can stay with Shirley until I heal."

"Or you can stay here."

"For six weeks? I couldn't do that. You don't even know me. I'll—"

"Red wine is supposed to be good for anemia, too. Would you like some?"

"I don't drink."

"I rarely do, myself." He turned his attention to his food for a few minutes, then said quietly, "Tell me about Tom."

Her fork paused midway to her mouth, then returned to her plate. "*He* drank." She pressed her napkin to her lips and took a deep breath. "I didn't mean to say that. It was just the first thing that popped into my mind.''

''Did he have a problem?''

''On the night of his accident, he'd been watching the World Series with some of his buddies, and he'd had a few too many beers. He ran into a concrete bridge barrier on his way home.''

''And was killed?''

She shook her head. ''He broke his neck. He died of pneumonia just over a year later.''

''I'm sorry.''

''Thank you.'' She tried to eat more, but the liver stuck in her throat. She put down her fork and said, ''I can't eat another bite.''

''Not even dessert?''

She smiled. ''Not even if it's chocolate.''

''I think it's something made with dried apricots. They're—''

''Very rich in iron,'' she finished for him, laughing.

''Tell me more about Tom,'' he said. ''What did he do?''

''Before the accident, you mean?''

Smith nodded.

''He ran a small computer-repair shop in Bartlesville—that's where we lived. He was a genius when it came to computers. And we had a small farm with a garden and an orchard. He loved to grow things. He could stick anything in the ground and make it grow, even roses. We had a beautiful bed by the front porch. And he loved to ride his horse. Not being able to ride his horse was—''

Jessica stopped as a flood of painful memories washed over her. She took a ragged breath. "Sorry, but I'm very tired. Would you excuse me, please?" She pushed her chair back and awkwardly tried to stand.

Smith rushed to her side and helped her up. "My apologies. I should have realized that you weren't up to a long evening. But as you can imagine, I'm very interested in this man who looked so much like me. Let me help you inside."

She didn't argue. She was tired, and talking about Tom was the last thing she wanted to do. Her life with him was behind her; she'd dealt with all the anger and sorrow long ago.

As he helped her inside, he said, "I hope you can forgive another question or two about your husband. What about his family? Do they live in Bartlesville?"

"There was only his mother and his grandmother. His mother died several years ago. His grandmother is in a nursing home with advanced Alzheimer's. I try to visit her when I can, but she doesn't recognize me anymore. Sometimes she calls me Ruth. That was Tom's mother."

"I see." When they reached the bed, he said, "Let me call Kathy."

"I can manage okay, thanks."

"You sure?"

"I'm sure."

Almost reluctantly, he left the room. She could sense that he wanted to ask more about Tom, and she couldn't blame him, but she just wasn't up to dredging up the past. It was bad enough that she had to look at Tom's likeness every time she looked at Smith. Smith was older, of course, but they could have passed for brothers. Twins almost.

Now that she had been around Smith more, she realized that he and Tom were very different. Their carriage was different, their demeanor…it was hard to describe. She rubbed her forehead. And thinking about it made her head hurt. Tomorrow she'd be stronger, and she would be on her way.

In his study, Smith sat staring at the photograph on his computer screen, the photograph of Tom and Jessica. He'd scanned it onto his machine. In fact, he'd copied every scrap of information he could find in Jessica's wallet and in her briefcase, down to her library card.

With a few clicks of the mouse, he found a telephone listing in Bartlesville for M.C. and Shirley Miles, and another for Miles Upholstery. That part of her story checked out. If Jessica was running some sort of scam, it was an elaborate one.

No, the more he was around her, the less likely it was that she was a scam artist. He was a pretty good judge of character, and he figured that she was exactly who she said she was.

He called up the photograph again and stared at it. "Are you my cousin?" he said aloud. "Could you be…my *brother?* Your name is Smith. My name is Smith. What's the connection?" His mother had told him that she'd named him Smith because of a movie she saw with a dashing hero named Smith. Now he wondered.

He turned his chair away from the screen and stared into nothingness. His brother? Kyle Rutledge was supposed to be his brother.

But he wasn't.

Four

Until recently, Smith hadn't seen any of his family in more than three years. He wouldn't have seen any of them then except that Kyle had come barging into his office one morning last month and caught him off guard.

"Mr. Rutledge," his secretary had said, "your brother is here to see you."

Smith's grip had tightened on the receiver when he'd heard that. "My brother?"

"Says he's your brother. Dr. Kyle Rutledge. Tall, blond, good-looking devil, killer smile. Shall I send him in?"

Scowling, Smith had hesitated. He could hear Kyle chuckling in the background. Damn Irma for her sassy ways. If she hadn't been so exceptional at keeping his office running smoothly, he'd have fired her on the spot. Since Kyle had known that he was in, there was nothing to do but see him.

"Send him in," Smith said. Slamming down the phone, he opened the middle drawer of his enormous desk and raked in the paper clips he'd been stringing. Since he'd lost interest in the corporation, he'd turned the reins over to a new CEO and kicked himself upstairs to chairman of the board. There really wasn't much to keep him occupied at the office anymore.

Kyle came in grinning like a possum.

"What the devil are you doing in town?" Smith asked.

"You don't return your messages, and I came to see if you were still alive. Man, it's good to see you." Kyle held out his hand, but when Smith took it, his brother pulled him into his arms in a bear hug, slapping him on the back and laughing. "It's been too long."

Smith tried to stay reserved, but he was glad to see the man he'd grown up with. He hugged Kyle back, and his grin was broad, too. "That it has. How's life treating the famous plastic surgeon?"

"Well. Very well. Irish and I can't complain. The new practice in Dallas is going great, and we have a son on the way."

"A son? Hey, that's fantastic. Sit down and tell me about your new wife. Sorry I missed your wedding. I had to be in China. Couldn't get out of it. You know how business is sometimes."

Kyle frowned and sat down in one of the plush

chairs across from Smith's desk. "I thought you were in the hospital. Motorcycle accident, as I recall."

"I guess maybe I was. It was Cousin Matt's wedding that I missed because of the China trip. Want a cup of coffee?"

Kyle shook his head. "I had too much on the plane."

"Orange juice? Or how about some grapefruit juice?"

"Nothing, thanks. Nothing, that is, except for some answers."

"About what?" Smith tried to act casual, but his guts were twisted in knots. He didn't want to have this conversation with Kyle.

"About what's going on with you and the family. For the past three years nobody has seen hide nor hair of you. You don't call, you don't write, you don't show up at any of the family gatherings. You send presents and flowers at the appropriate times, but otherwise it's as if you've disowned us. Grandpa Pete is worried, and though Dad makes excuses for you, I can tell he's worried, too. And every time your name is mentioned, Mama gets teary-eyed and fluttery and leaves the room. What's up, Smith?"

"Nothing's up," Smith said, shrugging as he lied through his teeth. "I just stay occupied with the business. It takes a hell of a lot of time to run one of the biggest computer companies in the world—to say nothing of the citrus groves. I have a lot of demands on my time. Smith Corp alone employs hundreds of people. It's the biggest single employer in this part of Texas."

Kyle grinned. "You don't have to sell me on your company. I bought stock when it went public."

"You did?"

"Yep. And I was hoping that you'd have more time when you became chairman of the board a few months ago and let somebody else take over as CEO."

"It's eased up some, but I still stay swamped."

"I know Mom and Dad would appreciate a simple phone call now and then. Grandpa Pete, too. I know that I'd like to hear from you, Smith. We used to be close. What happened?"

"Life, Kyle. Life happened. Things aren't as simple as they were when we were kids."

"Don't I know it. Say, you have time for lunch with your brother? We've got a lot of catching up to do, and I have a four o'clock flight back to Dallas."

Smith checked his watch. "Sure, I can arrange it. Let me call my housekeeper, and we can go out to my place for a bite. You can see the groves and my horses."

After a quick tour of the company, Smith had driven Kyle out to Sugartime, and, for a couple of hours they had been brothers again, reminiscing, joking and laughing, catching up on lost time.

When lunch was over, Kyle leaned back in his chair on the veranda. "I take it you're hooked on the Valley."

Smith propped his boots on the railing, shrugged and said, "I like it well enough."

"Nice house you have here. Kind of reminds me of the one Jackson bought in Austin." Jackson and

Matt Crow were first cousins to the Rutledge boys and as close as brothers when they were growing up.

"Jackson's in Austin?"

"Yep. He's on the railroad commission."

"*Jackson?* He never struck me as the public-spirited type."

Kyle laughed. "He's in love. It makes us all do strange things. I look for him to get married pretty soon. Soon as he can talk Olivia into it. Seems like all of Cherokee Pete's grandsons have taken the fall, except you, Smith. Or have you? Is that why we haven't seen much of you?"

Smith shook his head. "I don't have much time for romance." He checked his watch. "I'd better get you back to town if you're going to make your flight."

They drove to Harlingen to drop Kyle off at his rental car.

In the parking lot, Kyle hesitated before he got out. "I'm not sure I know much more than I did before I came—except that you're obviously healthy. I know that something is wrong, but I can't help unless I know what it is, Smith. Any time you want to talk, give me a call." He handed him a business card. "That has my home phone, office phone and cell phone numbers on it. You can reach me at any hour." He clapped Smith's thigh. "I love you, little brother. Always have, always will. Get in touch with Mom now and then."

Smith clamped his teeth together and gave a curt nod. He hadn't dared say more.

Kyle left then, and Smith waved as the rental

pulled away. Standing there watching as the car disappeared, he'd felt a hole in his heart as big as Texas. And sad. Damn, he'd felt sad. That sadness had dogged him till yet.

He'd been tempted to spill the whole business to Kyle, but he hadn't wanted to put him in the middle of it.

It would have been so simple. He only had to ask Kyle his blood type—though he already knew—and tell him his. Kyle was AB negative, just like his father. The two of them had always been popular at the blood bank because of their rare type. Smith was O positive, a more common type that he'd always assumed he shared with his mother. Except that he'd discovered three years ago that this wasn't so.

His mother was A negative.

There was no way that Smith could be Kyle's brother or his parents' son. No way in hell. He'd talked to a dozen experts in the field. Genetically, it was impossible for Smith to be related by blood to any of his so-called family.

He trudged back to his office, feeling worse after Kyle's visit than he had in all the months before. Kyle's coming had brought it all back—not that it was ever very far from the surface.

Irma looked up from her keyboard as he walked past. "'Afternoon, Mr. Rutledge. Hope you had a great lunch. You know, it's hard to believe that Dr. Rutledge is your brother. You don't look a thing alike. His hair is blond, and yours is auburn. His eyes are blue, and yours are green. Your builds are completely diff—''

"He favors his father," Smith said gruffly.

"Then you must take after your mother," Irma said.

"Who knows?" He'd strode to his office and slammed the door behind him.

Smith hadn't seen or talked to Kyle or any of the others since that day.

He didn't have any idea who his birth parents were, and he couldn't get anything out of the pair who'd raised him. Oh, he'd tried, but when he'd broached the subject with his mother, she'd denied vehemently that he was adopted. Three years before, when presented with indisputable evidence that he couldn't have been born to Dr. T. J. and Sarah Rutledge, he had again confronted his parents. His mother started crying, and his father threatened to punch him out for upsetting her.

Smith had quietly gone to both Grandpa Pete and his aunt Anna Crow, Jackson and Matt's mother. Both of them denied knowing anything about Smith's being adopted. They, too, joined the conspiracy of silence about his true origins.

In fact, Anna had told him that his notion about being adopted was nonsense. "Of course Sarah is your natural mother, Smith. I visited her in St. Louis when she was six months pregnant with you, and I still have the announcement of your birth three months after that. It's in a scrapbook in the den."

Despite what his aunt said, he knew that the story of his birth had been an elaborate deception. He had the documents to prove it. The facts were incontrovertible.

For thirty-four years he'd lived a lie. Smith couldn't face living that lie any longer, so he didn't go home anymore. He didn't go to his parents' house for Christmas or to Kyle's wedding in Ohio or to Matt's in Dallas. He'd sent extravagant gifts for every occasion along with his excuses, but he hadn't talked to any of them. He hadn't even talked to Cherokee Pete, that crusty old man that he adored, after Pete had refused to tell him the truth. His place in the family was irrevocably changed; he didn't belong. He didn't know who he was anymore.

And the only people who knew wouldn't tell him.

He stared again at the picture of Jessica and Tom on his computer screen. No, Kyle Rutledge wasn't his brother, but even Irma wouldn't have a problem figuring out that Tom Smith could be. The resemblance was too remarkable to be coincidental, and he'd examined that photograph carefully from every angle. It wasn't faked. It was real. Somehow, he and Tom Smith were related. They had to be.

Family. He's part of my real family, Smith thought. Illogical as it seemed, he *knew* it, felt it deep inside some part of himself. "And dammit! I'm too late!"

He slammed the heel of his hand against the screen, then rose and strode from the house.

At the stables, he saddled Rio and rode through the groves, not stopping until the horse and he were worn out.

Jessica O'Connor Smith held the key to his past. He was as sure of it as he ever had been of anything.

This time he meant to have some answers. He wasn't giving up until he knew all there was to know.

She couldn't tie her own damn sneakers! Frustrated, Jessica threw one of the shoes across the room just as Kathy opened the door.

"Oops!" the nurse said as a sneaker sailed past her. "Having a tantrum, are we?"

Jessica laughed. "You got it. Have you ever tried to tie laces with only one hand?"

"It's a pain, I know. I'll pick up some sandals or slip-ons today for you. That should make it easier. And Rosa or I will be glad to help you dress."

"I hate depending on anyone. And I certainly don't need a nurse—not that I haven't appreciated all you've done, Kathy—but I'm fine now. Well, almost fine."

"I understand. I don't think you need me either, but Mr. Rutledge seems determined for me to stay another few days at least. And at the wages he's paying, I hope you'll put up with me for a while longer." She grinned. "I can just about pay for my oldest daughter's college tuition next year. Sit down and I'll fix your hair again. You look as if you had a restless night."

"Um." She sat down while Kathy tackled her curly mop. Yes, she'd had a very restless night, plagued by strange feelings about Smith Rutledge. He had so many of the qualities that she'd loved about Tom—and none of the bad. It was almost as if Smith was what Tom could have been if he hadn't taken the wrong fork in the road. Old sensations, potent and visceral, had been stirred as well. Smith was a very sexy man...and she'd been celibate—for a long, long time.

"Tell me what you know about Smith," Jessica said.

"Besides that he's rich?"

"Yes, besides that."

"I really don't know anything about his personal life—just things I read in the paper. Having his company locate here gave a big boost to the economy around Harlingen. He donates to lots of causes—everything from Boy Scouts to cancer research. But I'm sure that you know all that."

"Not really. I actually don't know much about him at all."

Kathy frowned and was about to say something when there was a knock at the door.

"Yes?" Jessica called.

Smith stuck in his head. She was startled anew at his resemblance to Tom. Each time she saw him, she had to remind herself that he wasn't Tom come to life, but some sort of cosmic fluke. Still, it was unnerving.

"Are you ready for breakfast?" he asked.

"She's ready," Kathy said, sticking in the last pin and giving her braid a pat. "There you go."

Jessica rose, smoothed her T-shirt over her shorts and joined him. "I'm not much for breakfast, but I'd love a cup of coffee." She turned to Kathy. "Join us?"

"No, thanks. I've eaten already, and I have an errand."

Smith touched his hand to her back to escort her, and a strange ripple skittered up her spine. An odd reaction—though she had to admit that the man was not only very good-looking but also exuded an aura of some sort that was downright magnetizing. She'd always been attracted to Tom's rugged handsomeness, the same chiseled features that Smith possessed, but Tom had lacked that elusive quality that Smith seemed to have in bushels—a kind of sex appeal that came with confidence and success. Tom had always had a sort of beaten-down air about him, not cowed certainly, but more like a resigned-to-his-fate-but-pissed-about-it attitude.

Smith ushered her to a table set up by the pool in the back. Bowls of fresh strawberries awaited them, along with large glasses of orange juice.

When she was seated, she glanced around for a coffeepot. "No coffee?" she asked.

"We'll have some later. The nutritionist said that caffeine could interfere with iron absorption."

She cocked an eyebrow. "Maybe so, but it does wonders for my temperament. I don't function well until I've had several cups of coffee."

"We'll have some after we eat."

"Lord, you're bossy."

He laughed. "You got that right. Eat your strawberries. And you can have bran flakes with raisins and walnuts or a ham-and-cheese omelette."

"I'd prefer a doughnut and a cup of coffee."

He grinned. "Not a choice."

"Cereal then. Just sprinkle on some iron shavings

with the sugar.'' She dug into the strawberries, which were excellent.

"I made a long-distance call on your phone," she said between bites. "I hope you don't mind. My cell phone is out of juice and I needed to touch base with Shirley. She worries."

"Your partner?"

Jessica nodded. "I'll pay for the call."

"That won't be necessary."

She started to argue, then changed her mind and concentrated on her food.

Later, when she had finished every last raisin and walnut at the bottom of the bowl, Smith poured a cup of coffee from the carafe that Ric had left. "Ah, heaven. Thanks."

They drank their coffee without conversation, and she studied him carefully. Smith was more muscular than Tom, but he had the same square jaw and deep cleft in his chin, the same coloring, the same eyes. His hair was fuller and had a better cut, but it was the same wiry auburn hair that Tom had always complained about. And his voice—she could have closed her eyes and sworn it was Tom. They were so alike, yet she had already seen huge differences between them as well.

Smith poured a second cup, he leaned back and said, "Tell me some more about him."

"About who?"

"Tom. I could tell you were thinking about him, comparing us."

"What would you like to know?"

"About his mother and how he grew up, about who his father was, that sort of thing."

Jessica sat back in her chair and stared at the sun glistening on the pool water for a moment, then said, "He never knew who his father was. His mother wouldn't talk about it. After she died, when he was about seven, he went to Bartlesville to live with his grandmother. When Tom asked her about his father, all she would say is he was 'one of them hippies she run off and lived with, God only knew which piece of trash done the deed.'"

Smith winced. "What an awful thing to tell a kid."

"Grandma Lula was a bitter, mean-spirited old woman. Tom would have been better off raised in a foster home like I was."

"You grew up in a foster home?"

She nodded. "From the time I was in the fourth grade. I guess that's one of the things that drew Tom and me together—alcoholic mothers who died or abandoned us. My foster parents helped me overcome my past. Tom's grandmother harped on his constantly."

"His mother was alcoholic?"

"Yes, and worse. Drugs, I think. Tom didn't like to talk about it, but from what little he told me, they lived on welfare and moved around, so that he didn't go to school much. He was hungry a lot of the time." She glanced at Smith and found that his mouth was a grim line and his hand was rubbing his forehead. "At least his grandmother fed him and sent him to school. Tom was very bright."

"Did he go to college?"

"He got an associates degree from the local junior college. He worked and took night classes mostly. I tried to get him to go on and get a four-year degree, but by then he already had his own business, and he said he was too old. And by that time, we were engaged."

"How long were you married?"

"Seven years. We had dated since I was in high school, but we agreed that I should finish college before we got married. The day after I graduated, we had the ceremony in the church parlor. Shirley and her husband were our attendants. It wasn't much of a wedding, and we could only afford a weekend in Tulsa for a honeymoon, but we were happy...then. I have a picture in my wallet—"

"I've seen it. He was...how old when you married?"

"Oh, let's see, I was twenty-two, and he must have been twenty-eight."

Smith went very still. Those familiar eyes bored into hers. "How old was Tom when he died?"

Jessica looked away. She didn't want to talk about Tom, to dredge up all those years again, but something in Smith's tone made her answer. "Thirty-five. Just thirty-five. He looked twenty years older. That year after the accident was very hard on him."

"And he died when?"

"Two years ago last Christmas."

"That would have made him—" Smith was looking at her very strangely, so strangely that a shiver rippled up her spine. "When was his birthday?" he asked sharply.

"June the sixteenth."

Smith paled. His cup clattered in his saucer.

Five

Smith felt as if a house had fallen on him. How could this be?

"What's wrong?" Jessica asked.

"June sixteenth is *my* birthday. And I'm thirty-seven years old."

"But—but that would make you—"

"Twins." Swallowing lye wouldn't have burned a bigger hole in his gut. For a minute, his brain wouldn't function. Then he said sharply, too sharply from the expression on her face, "Give me the exact dates of Tom's accident and his death."

As soon as she gave him the information, he stood. "If you'll excuse me, Kathy and Rosa will take care of anything you need."

He knew she had questions, but he wasn't ready

to talk. He had to digest all this first. And he had to check it out. Nobody had ever accused Smith Rutledge of being a fool. Yet, even as he strode toward his study and his computer, he knew. He *knew*. He'd known most of his life that a part of him was missing.

It didn't take him long to verify that a Thomas Edward Smith did die that day in Oklahoma. But he wanted details that weren't directly available online. He made a couple of phone calls and within an hour he had an e-mail with copies of several columns from the Bartlesville newspaper, including Tom's obituary, which listed his date of birth and his survivors as wife, Jessica O'Connor Smith, and grandmother, Lula Jane Smith. M. C. "Mack" Miles was listed as a pallbearer.

An article about the accident showed a mangled motorcycle and mentioned that Thomas Smith, local businessman, was returning home from a party at a friend's house. And, son of a bitch, he hadn't been wearing a helmet.

Smith dropped his head in his hands and cursed again. He'd crashed his motorcycle, too. About the time Kyle got married. A drunk driver had veered across the median and hit him head-on. But Smith had been wearing a helmet. He'd gotten bunged up a little, but Tom had broken his neck. He'd been flown to Tulsa in critical condition.

For several minutes, he sat staring out the window at the groves, watching the wind sway the limbs. His mind raced, examining a dozen possibilities, mulling over the information, trying to make sense of it all. If, indeed, he and Tom were twins, how did they get separated?

Damn his parents for not telling him the truth! If he'd known ten years ago—hell, if they'd told him just a few weeks before the accident, when he'd asked three years ago, Tom might still be alive. His life would have been different.

He cursed some more, loud and long.

Finally, he turned back to the screen and scrolled through other articles: the announcement of Tom and Jessica's wedding along with the picture she carried in her wallet, a picture with a short article on Jessica's winning an award for teacher of the year, two others with Jessica and her students in art shows. The last was an article written two and a half years before. Teachers at the junior-high school were having a bake sale to raise money for Tom's extensive medical bills and treatments.

A bake sale? Dammit! A *bake* sale?

He rose and strode from the room.

If Jessica was shaken, she could only imagine how Smith must feel. She wanted to go to him and comfort him, talk to him, ease the pain he must be feeling. But if he was anything like Tom, she knew that he wouldn't appreciate the gesture. Maybe it was a male thing, but Tom never wanted to talk about matters that troubled him. He shut her out. He went off and brooded alone. And drank. He'd brooded and drank a lot. That was why she'd left him.

* * *

If Smith had been a drinking man, he'd have gotten drunk. Instead, he saddled Rio and rode all morning. Then he went to the gym over the garage and pumped iron until his muscles trembled from exhaustion. His head still about to explode, he made for the pool. Stripping off shoes and shorts, he dived in and began swimming laps.

Jessica stood behind the sheer curtains and watched him swim. She'd counted twenty laps of the long pool, and he showed no signs of stopping. His muscled arms sliced through the water with ease. She'd been about to go outside and get some sun when she'd seen him stalk to the deep end and shuck his clothes. As an art major and a long-married woman, she was no stranger to the nude male form, but Smith was no ordinary male. He had the body of a Greek Olympian.

Her breath had caught at the sight of him.

Hard. Muscled. Magnificent.

For propriety's sake, she should have turned away. She didn't. Mesmerized by his tanned body, she had stood rooted there and watched as he undressed and dived in the water. He hadn't noticed her, so she simply took a few steps back until she was hidden by the sheers drawn across half of the sliding glass door.

Although their builds were roughly the same, at least clothed, there was a world of difference between Smith's body and Tom's. Even in the early days of their marriage, Jessica couldn't recall being so...breathless over Tom's body. A low, sweet ache began to unfurl inside her. Heat flushed over her face. Dear God, she was getting turned on just watching him swim.

Feeling like a voyeuristic fool, she forced herself to turn away and retreat to her room. Things were getting too complicated around here. The sooner she left this house, the better.

She had urgent business in Matamoros.

Jessica didn't see Smith again until breakfast the next morning by the pool. Although he was scrupulously polite, he said little as they ate. Every time she looked at him, flashes of him standing nude played havoc with her mind, so she kept her gaze on her plate.

It didn't help. Hadn't she been obsessing about him half the night?

This was ridiculous! All she had to do was announce to Smith Rutledge that she had work to do and leave.

But she couldn't seem to get the words out. Instead she kept shoveling omelette into her mouth.

When the meal was finished, Smith poured coffee for them both.

"I've verified—"

"I'm leaving—" she blurted out at the same time he spoke.

"Sorry," he said. "Go ahead."

Why was she so unnerved? She'd never had a problem expressing herself. "I was going to say that while I appreciate all that you've done for me, I have work to do, and I'm leaving today. I'm—"

"No," he said quietly, "you're not."

"Yes," she said emphatically, "I am. I have to try to keep the business dates I've scheduled, and I need to make a trip to Matamoros right away. It's very important that I locate a woman there, and I can hire a driver for the trip. I made a few phone calls yesterday afternoon, and I found—"

"What is so critical about finding some woman in Matamoros?"

"Her name is Mrs. Lopez, and she's the aunt of Carmen, a woman who used to work in Mack's upholstery shop. She did the beadwork on the silk panels we use on some of our evening bags, and it's exquisite. It's also affordable. We've run out of our stock, and I need to contract with her to make some more. Carmen moved, and we haven't been able to contact either her or the aunt by phone or by mail. We're hoping that if I go there, I can locate Mrs. Lopez. I have her old address. We figured that maybe some of her neighbors might know how to find her."

"Do you speak Spanish?"

"Only a few words. But the places that I called about a driver—"

"If you're so hell-bound to go, I'll take you. Matamoros is a very large city, and parts of it aren't safe for a woman alone—especially one who doesn't speak the language."

"But I'm sure that you have more important things to do than chauffeur me around."

"Nope. Not a thing. When do you want to leave?"

She glanced at her watch. "Darn it!"

"A problem?"

"My watch stopped."

"You need a new battery?"

"Probably, but a battery costs about as much as the watch. Maybe I can pick up another one at Wal-Mart while we're out."

"Or in Mexico. You can get some deals across the border on knockoffs. Can you be ready in an hour?"

Conceding that he was determined to take her, she sighed. "I can be ready in fifteen minutes."

They talked more about Tom on the way to the border. Smith wanted to know every detail of his life. After she'd talked for several minutes, she asked, "Didn't your parents mention that you had a twin? I wonder why they didn't adopt both of you."

She saw Smith's knuckles go white as they gripped the wheel. "They told me nothing. I didn't even know I was adopted until three years ago. And my family still won't admit that I wasn't born to Sarah Rutledge."

"Dear Lord! How terrible. How did you find out that she wasn't your birth mother?"

He related the story. "But even with irrefutable evidence, they wouldn't back down and tell me the truth."

"Did your parents ever mistreat you when you were growing up?"

"God, no. They were great parents. I never doubted that they loved my brother Kyle and me, and there was no difference in the way they raised the two of us. I had a fantastic childhood—everything a kid could want."

"Then count your blessings, Smith. Take it from me, it's hard on a child to grow up abused and neglected. Tom or I would have traded places with you in a heartbeat. For whatever reason that your folks kept your adoption a secret, it's history now. Forget it. Put it behind you and move on. As my foster father always told me, 'Looking back too much will only give you a crick in your neck.'"

"Sounds like my Grandpa Pete—a real folksy type always ready with an adage for every occasion."

She almost shot back a cheeky reply, then thought better of it and kept her mouth shut. He was hurting, and she knew it.

They were quiet for several miles. Only the whine of the tires on the road broke the heavy silence. It was obvious that he was nursing a major grudge against his parents that was only making matters worse, but she also knew that anything she said to him wouldn't do any good. Why were men so darned stubborn?

Soon they were in Brownsville and crossing the bridge over the Rio Grande into Mexico. Although Brownsville and Matamoros abutted, it was immediately evident that they were in another country. Besides the signs being in Spanish, there was a different air about the large, bustling city. Since, except for a street name and number, she didn't have a clue where they were going, she was grateful for Smith's presence.

He stopped once and spoke to a man in rapid Spanish, asking directions, he said. As they moved off the main thoroughfares, the streets became poorer and poorer and the houses were little more than shacks thrown together with scraps of this and that.

"This is the squatters' area," Smith told her. "People move here from the interior of Mexico, where conditions are even worse, and build a house of some sort on a small parcel of land. If they live here for five years, then the land becomes theirs."

He pulled to a stop in front of a small grocery store where a group of men had congregated and spoke to them in Spanish. After a few moments of conversation and some pointing, he said, *"Gracias,"* and pulled away.

"The address is on the next block."

But Señora Lopez didn't live there anymore. Her son and his family, with whom she had lived, had moved to another town, but they did learn that the woman, now living with her daughter and her family, was only a few blocks away.

When they finally located Señora Lopez, the old woman, her hands gnarled with arthritis, was ecstatic to learn that Jessica wanted to hirc her. From the poor condition of their tiny house, it was obvious that the family was barely eking out a living. With Smith interpreting, they made a deal for the beadwork. Jessica left the designs and presorted packages of raw materials with Mrs. Lopez and her daughter, who was anxious to help. She had given the women a small advance and made arrangements for the shipping of finished pieces as well as for receiving new materials.

As they drove away, Jessica said, "Remind me to

never again complain about having to live on a tight budget. How do all these people survive?''

''It's hard,'' Smith said. ''And there's no welfare in Mexico. The money the women make from doing your beadwork will support the whole family.''

Jessica worried her lip. ''The price we agreed on for the pieces seems very cheap. Maybe I should have offered her more.''

''No, actually, your offer was very generous, equal to about triple the minimum wage here.''

''Unbelievable.''

They drove to a more prosperous-looking area of the city and Smith parked in front of a jewelry shop. ''We can get your watch here.''

When they went inside, Smith spoke affably with the proprietor of the very nice store. The man seemed overjoyed to see Smith, frisking about like a nervous puppy and smiling broadly.

After looking around for only a moment Jessica leaned close to Smith and said out of the corner of her mouth, ''I think their merchandise is too rich for my blood. This looks like the real stuff.''

''Most of it is the real stuff, but they have the knockoff versions as well. A lot of the time, you can't tell it from the real McCoy—until your wrist starts to turn green.'' He grinned, then spoke to the proprietor in that rapid-fire Spanish that amazed her—and was certainly beyond her limited vocabulary.

When the man went through a rear door, she asked, ''What did you say?''

"I told him that we wanted to look at some of his best fake watches. He keeps them in the back."

The shop owner soon returned with a tray of exquisite women's watches—all recognizable high-end name brands. Jessica almost drooled over them. "These are gorgeous. They can't be fake."

"You can take your pick for nineteen ninety-five. And I understand that they really keep pretty good time, too."

With Smith's help, she tried on half a dozen. "I can't decide between the Rolex and the Piaget." She held out her arm. "What do you think?"

"Why don't you get them both?"

"Because even at a bargain, it's an extravagance I can't afford. I'll take the one with the stretch band. It will be easier with my cast."

Smith tried to pay for the watch, but Jessica insisted on putting the charges on her credit card. While Smith and the owner concluded the deal in Spanish, she wandered around the store, looking longingly at lovely gold earrings and diamond rings. She didn't have any real jewelry of her own left—not that she'd ever had much, but she didn't even have her engagement or wedding ring anymore. She'd sold them long ago.

They stopped for lunch at a very nice restaurant, then wandered around in the open marketplace for a while before they headed home.

"Thanks for going with me," Jessica told him as they drove back across the bridge. "I would have been lost if I'd gone by myself."

"I was glad to help."

She held up her arm to admire the new watch. "I can't get over how great this looks. It would fool anybody."

"You should have bought the other one as well."

"No way. I know you don't understand tight budgets, but I'm on one. I can't afford two watches— even at nineteen ninety-five. And that's why I need to get back to work."

"You need to take time off to let your wrist heal and get your anemia under control."

"But dammit, can't you understand that I can't *afford* to take time off? I have to make a go of this business. I'm knee-deep in—" She stopped herself before she said more. Her debts were none of his business.

"Knee-deep in what?"

"Nothing."

"In debt?"

"Look," she said, "I'm not whining about it. I simply have obligations that I must meet."

"What kind of obligations?"

She didn't want to tell him about the huge medical expenses for Tom that she was still paying off, but he kept grilling her until she blurted out the whole thing. "My insurance from the school covered a lot of the costs, but not nearly all of them. That's one of the reasons I wanted to go into business. I believe in our products, and I know that if I work hard and keep my expenses low, I can make enough to pay off all those bills in a couple of years. It would have taken forever on my teacher's salary. I've given myself a year to make a go of the handbag lines, so you see it's critical that I keep to my schedule. And the Dallas show can make or break us.''

"Let me help," he said.

"I'm not looking for charity, thankyouvery-much.''

Smith pulled into the parking lot of a strip center and turned to her. "Jessica, I know that Tom was my brother. It tears my guts out that I was never able to know him. I've got more money than I can spend in ten lifetimes. Let me do this for Tom. It means a lot to me.''

She studied his face. There was no doubting his sincerity. She knew that it was important to him. And letting him take the terrible financial burden off her shoulders was a sensible solution to her problem. But she'd always been a giver, not a taker. Independent. Self-sufficient. Mel, her foster father, had told her dozens of times that she needed to learn to let go of her stiff-necked pride and simply say "thank you" when somebody tried to help. She could almost hear Mel's voice whispering in her ear now. *Let somebody who needs to give have the opportunity*.

"All right," she finally said. "Thank you."

"Good. Now that's settled. You can concentrate on healing.''

"Not exactly. I agreed that you can pay Tom's medical bills. I still have a partner and a business to build. And I still have a cash-flow problem. I need the sales from Corpus Christi and Houston to finance the stock for Dallas. And I'll probably have to hire—"

Smith rolled his eyes heavenward. "God, you're stubborn, woman!"

"*I'm* stubborn?"

"Class A mule-headed. Listen, will you concede that I know a thing or two about business?"

"Of course."

"An important business principle is to establish contacts and use those contacts to get a leg up."

"I know that. That's what I've been busting my butt to do. That's why I'm calling on boutiques and displaying in booths every chance I get."

"And I'm sure that you've been doing a good job, but I'm probably the best business contact you've made. Let me help you."

"How?"

"I'll have to think on it some, but for starters, how many of those back bags do you plan to sell at the fair in Corpus?"

"Seventy-five if I'm lucky."

"I'll buy a hundred, and you can cancel the Corpus gig at least."

"But what are you going to do with a hundred bags?"

He started the SUV and pulled out of the parking lot. "Give them as Christmas gifts to some of my employees."

"But it's only February."

"I like to shop early and beat the crowds."

"I can't believe that you said that with a straight face. Anyway, the fair isn't the only reason I'm going to Corpus. I need to call on boutiques there to show them our line of evening bags."

"How about I make a phone call and introduce you to Sandi instead?"

"Who's Sandi?"

"The wife of Brandan Myers, one of my college roommates." He grinned. "And a buyer for Neiman's."

Six

Jessica couldn't sleep. She was too excited. *Neiman Marcus!* Imagine. Smith had phoned his old buddy, Brandan Myers, and, in turn, had spoken with his former roommate's wife, Sandi.

"She wants you to send her slides of some of your samples," Smith had told Jessica. "Do you have any slides?"

"Lord, no," she said, suddenly anxious. "It never occurred to us to have any made. Naive, I suppose, but we're new at this business and learning as we go along. What can I do?"

Smith had hurriedly arranged for a photographer from the media department at Smith Corp to do a little moonlighting. Over the weekend, they had a set of very classy slides made and overnighted to Sandi's office in Dallas.

After three days of nail-biting, Jessica had received a call from Sandi. The buyer had liked what she'd seen. Could she come in with samples? For sure, even if she had to hitchhike to Dallas—though she didn't say anything so crass aloud. She'd played it super cool and businesslike and didn't scream until she hung up the phone.

And now it was set. She had an appointment with a buyer for Neiman's on Monday! Never in their wildest dreams had she and Shirley envisioned their evening bags selling at the ritzy stores. It was too much to hope for.

She didn't know if she could stand the suspense for another five days. Should she call Shirley and tell her the news? But what if Sandi Myers didn't like their designs when she saw the real thing? What if Jessica was just getting her hopes up for nothing?

What if—

She tossed and turned, trying to get comfortable with her cast and squelch the what-ifs buzzing in her head.

It was no use. She threw back the covers and got out of bed. Maybe a glass of milk would help. And a cookie. Or two. Or three. Rosa had made some chocolate chip ones that were to die for. She considered putting on her robe, then decided against it. It was two-thirty in the morning; the house was quiet; everyone was asleep. She'd just sneak to the kitchen and be back in a flash.

The trip there was no problem. Carrying her snack back to her room would be tricky with the cast. She poured a glass of milk and wrapped three cookies in a paper towel, making a little bag of it so that she could carry it between her teeth. She turned off the light with her elbow and crept back along the dim hall, her bare feet silent on the tile.

Suddenly, she ran smack into a large obstacle. Startled, she let out a shriek, jumped back, and the cookies and milk crashed to the floor.

"What the—?" Smith flipped on a light. He wore only a half-zipped pair of jeans.

The glass was in a million pieces; milk was splattered all over the floor and soaked the front of her gown. The cookies and the paper towel had landed in the middle of the mess.

She felt like such an idiot standing there, like a kid caught in a naughty act. The look Smith gave her made her feel even worse. She could almost see his molars grinding as his gaze swept over her from head to bare toes to the disaster on the floor.

She stared at his naked chest while a tiny trickle of milk slowly ran down his breastbone over a thin scar, over his corded abdomen and into his navel. Unthinking, she dabbed at the drops with her fingers. The moment she touched his belly button, she realized what she'd done and jerked her hand away, mortified.

For several seconds there was total silence. Neither of them even breathed. A taut awareness hummed in the air like a struck tuning fork.

Laughing nervously, she said, "Sorry. I seem to have trouble holding on to food around you. I've made a mess. I'll clean it up."

"No!" he said, grabbing her shoulders. "Don't move. You'll cut your feet. I'll carry you."

She glanced down. "But what about you? You're not wearing shoes either."

"Wait here just a minute." He backed away, then strode down the hall toward his room.

Jessica felt like such an idiot. She started to tiptoe through the glass slivers anyhow, then thought better of it when she saw how many sharp pieces there were. And—dear Lord—she was horrified to see what the milk had done to her nightgown. The whole front of her gown was soaked and the silky fabric was plastered against her body like plastic wrap. No wonder Smith was gawking.

She grabbed a wet section and held it out, flapping it in a futile effort to dry the material.

Smith returned wearing loafers and, without a word, lifted her into his arms, crunched over the glass, and carried her into her bathroom before he set her on her feet. "You're soaked."

"Tell me something I don't know. Listen, I'm really sorry about the floor."

"Forget the floor. Did you hurt yourself? Is your cast okay?"

"I'm fine. The cast is fine. I just need to wash up a little."

She waited for him to leave. He didn't. Instead he turned on the water and grabbed a towel and a washcloth.

"What are you doing?" she squealed.

"I'm going to help you clean up. You can't do it by yourself. I knew we should have kept Kathy."

"I don't need a nurse anymore," she told him. "It's a foolish expense. And I may be a little slow, but I can clean up by myself." She grabbed the towel and held it in front of her, trying to preserve some modicum of modesty.

A hint of a smile flickered at the corner of his mouth. "It's too late."

"What's too late?"

"The towel."

She closed her eyes and willed herself to disappear into a crack in the floor. It didn't work. When she opened her eyes, they were both still standing there.

"Don't be stubborn," he said. "Let me help you."

"No. And it's not open to negotiation. But thank you."

Finally, he shook his head and left.

It took her half an hour to bathe and change. She was exhausted from the effort. Sleep wouldn't be hard now, she thought as she trudged from the bathroom into her bedroom.

She stopped. There, on the bedside table, sat a glass of milk and a plate of cookies. Her eyes misted.

"You dear, sweet man," she whispered.

If Smith had been restless before, he was like a fly in the glue jar now. The image of Jessica in that wet gown was burned into his brain. Dammit to hell, he was lusting after his brother's widow. It wasn't right. He felt like a mangy, low-down cur dog.

And horny as the devil.

He'd been thinking of Jessica a lot in the past few days, thinking of her in ways that he shouldn't have been. He'd memorized the scent of her. Her laughter echoed in his head; her face filled his mind. His hands itched to cup her breasts, mold her hips, spread her thighs. He couldn't remember when a woman had gotten under his skin the way Jessica had. Being with her long hours every day was wearing on him, and seeing her in that wet gown only added fuel to the fire smoldering inside.

Man, get a grip on, he told himself. *She's off-limits.*

He strode outside to the pool, stripped and dived in.

No matter how fast he swam, he couldn't escape the thoughts of her, the bone-deep aching that bedeviled him. He was asking for trouble keeping Jessica around, but he couldn't turn her out when she needed help. He owed it to the brother he never knew.

Somehow he would manage to keep his hands in his pockets and his thoughts to himself.

Somehow.

By the time Monday arrived, Jessica was a basket case. Rosa had helped her dress in her best suit, a designer classic that she'd found at a resale shop in Tulsa. The jacket sleeve wouldn't fit over her cast. She was almost in tears, when Smith intervened and convinced her to simply drape the jacket over her left shoulder and the sling.

They were about to leave the house, when she yelled, "Wait!" and ran back to her room. She grabbed one of the vials of perfume and hurried back to the door where he stood waiting.

"Would you open this for me?" She thrust the sample at him.

He opened the tiny vial and waited until she dabbed a bit behind her ears and at the V of her blouse. "Smells good," he said, recapping the bottle and dropping it into his pocket.

"It's my favorite. I've been saving the scent for a special occasion."

"Why don't you have a bigger bottle?"

"Because it costs the world. The little vials are free. Shirley and I made several trips to the mall to stock up for my trek. Believe me, buyers and boutique owners notice the quality of your dress." She held out her foot to display her pump. "These babies are outrageous if you pay regular retail. I got them at a discount place for almost nothing."

"You look nice. Very...prosperous."

"Thanks." She jiggled her good wrist. "Think she'd notice that my watch is a fake?"

"I doubt it," he said. "It's a very good copy."

He carried her leather coat, her briefcase and an exquisite black leather sample case that he'd scrounged up somewhere. It had wheels and a telescoping handle so that she could easily pull it and piggyback her briefcase for her appointment.

They drove to the airport, boarded a private company jet, and were at Love Field in Dallas with plenty of time to drive downtown in a chauffeured car for her eleven o'clock appointment. Now, *this* was the way to travel, Jessica thought as the large black sedan made its way through the traffic. *Don't get used to all this luxury,* she warned herself. Soon she'd be back to herding the old RV.

Smith was even ready to accompany her to Sandi's office, but when they reached the elevator, Jessica said, "I appreciate all the help you've given me. I really do. But I need to do the rest by myself." She was expecting an argument.

He only smiled. "I understand. I'll do some shopping and meet you back here."

She took a deep breath, stepped into the elevator and pushed the button for the ninth floor. A lot was riding on her meeting.

An hour later, Jessica rode down the same elevator. Smith was waiting for her, a small shopping bag in his hand.

"Well," he said, "how did it go?"

Trying desperately to keep her emotions in check, she said, "Let's get out of here before we discuss it. And hurry."

Smith grabbed her cases, and they walked quickly from the posh department store to where their car was waiting.

Once they were in the back seat and the door was closed, Jessica let out a loud, "Yahooo!" and threw herself into Smith's arms, laughing.

He began laughing, too. "I take it that it's a go."

"It's a go," she said, planting a big kiss on him. "She loved the bags! Said they were exquisite. And she ordered a hundred to start. A *hundred!* To *start.* Is that wild? And she was talking about Christmas catalogs and online possibilities. Shirley won't believe it. Jeez, *I* don't believe it." She impetuously kissed him again. "I have to call her right away." She dug through her briefcase for her cell phone.

"How about some lunch to celebrate?"

"You're on."

He took her to a very exclusive restaurant on Turtle Creek, and they ate something divine, though Jessica barely tasted it. She was floating.

"When is delivery?" Smith asked.

"I promised the first fifty right away, the second fifty in a month."

"Do you have that many in stock?"

Panic assaulted her. "Oh, Lord, I don't know. Yes. No. Oh, cripes, I don't think so." She looked down at her useless arm, and the panic doubled. "What if I don't? What am I going to do? I can't work like this." She grabbed his hand across the table.

He laid his other hand atop hers and squeezed it. "Don't worry about it, darlin'. You're an entrepreneur and the president of a company. Do what company presidents do—delegate."

She smiled sweetly. "Do you sew?"

He threw back his head and laughed.

"Seriously, who am I going to delegate to? And, oh, dear, I wonder if Señora Lopez will have those beaded panels ready in time."

"I'm sure she will. Let me give your personnel problems some thought. Finding good workers shouldn't be difficult. Want dessert?"

"Absolutely. Something positively decadent and

deliciously sinful,'' she said in a breathy tone, her tongue making a slow sweep of her lips.

He lifted an eyebrow, and the suggestive look he gave her made her go stone still. She grabbed her water glass, but her hand shook so badly that she put it back on the table.

Was he coming on to her or had she imagined it? Maybe she shouldn't have kissed him earlier. She hadn't really meant to. It had been totally spontaneous, part of the excitement of the moment. She ought to make that clear. Any notion of *that* sort of relationship was completely out of the question.

Or was it?

Smith was a very sexy man, and he turned her on like all get out. No denying the truth. Hadn't she spent hours fantasizing about his belly button? And his muscles. And his hands. And his mouth.

Funny, when she looked at Smith now, she didn't see Tom. She simply saw…Smith, a unique and extraordinary man. While there were superficial similarities, of course, they were very different people. Soul-deep different.

Perhaps…

Well, she would keep her options open.

As they left for the airport after lunch, Jessica admired the residential areas they passed through, the winding streets, the old oak trees. "This part of Dallas is quite beautiful."

He nodded. "I grew up not too far from here."

"You did? Do your parents still live nearby?"

"Yes. Let's talk about some options for a work-force."

"Don't you want to stop by for a visit since we're so close? I don't mind."

"I doubt that they're home."

"You could call."

"Another time," he said, obviously not wanting to pursue the subject.

"How long since you've been to see your parents?"

"A while. I think you have several ways to go on hiring help. You could have the bags made in Mexico, which would hold down costs, but having the work done across the border would require you to secure work facilities and live there for a while, or commute every day, until you trained a supervisor. Plus, there are the language problems. And the time constraints."

"I don't want to live in Mexico. My Spanish is abominable and commuting is a pain. How long is 'a while'?"

"Three years. Another option would be to set up a workshop in Harlingen and hire some local people. I'm sure Rosa could help us there. I think her sister is a seamstress."

"I like that idea better. You haven't seen your parents in *three* whole years?"

"No."

She started to say more, but he shot her that clenched-jaw expression, the mulish one that said he wasn't budging, so forget it. She dropped the subject, and they discussed workshops and personnel the rest of the way to the airport.

Was it her imagination or was Smith actually excited about helping her with the business? The notion seemed absurd. After all, he was head of a giant corporation, to say nothing of running the huge production of the farm. Why would he care about her small enterprise?

Maybe his involvement was because of Tom, his feeling that she was his family responsibility. Or maybe it was because he needed a new challenge. Whatever the reason, she was enormously grateful.

After they boarded the plane, she said, "I really haven't thanked you for your help in all this. What has happened today is beyond anything I could have hoped for. And none of it would have been possible without you. Thank you, Smith."

"*De nada.*" He winked, then buckled her seat belt.

When they were airborne, Jessica noticed the shopping bag in one of the seats. "Buy something interesting?"

"A gift." He opened the bag and pulled out a package wrapped in silver paper and tied with a blue bow. He handed it to her. "For you. To congratulate you on the big sale."

"But what if I hadn't made the sale?"

"Then it would have been a consolation prize."

She looked at the package for a long time. She couldn't remember the last time anyone had given her a gift when it wasn't Christmas or her birthday. She was very touched.

"Aren't you going to open it?"

Smiling, she tore off the bow and the paper. She found a bottle of her favorite perfume. A very large bottle.

She couldn't help herself. She hugged him again.

Seven

Too restless to read or watch TV and too excited to try to sleep, Jessica opened the door from her room and stepped outside into the glorious night. The moon was completely full, lighting the grounds and the groves, and the most delicious scents she'd ever smelled infused the air.

In the past two days, the grapefruit and orange trees had burst into bloom, and their honeysuckle-like fragrance perfumed the area for a half mile or more. She breathed in deeply, savoring the scent that played on the breeze and bathed her face.

"It's something, isn't it?"

Jolted by the sound of Smith's voice, she slapped her hand to her chest and turned quickly. "Oh, you scared me."

He moved from the shadows, farther down the long veranda that ran the length of the wing, and came toward her. "Sorry," he said. "I didn't mean to startle you. I was on my way out to the gym, and I stopped to smell the flowers."

He wore shorts, athletic shoes and a cropped T-shirt that bared his navel. A towel hung around his neck. She zeroed in on his navel. Why, of all the belly buttons she'd seen in her life, did his hold such a fascination for her? She didn't have a clue as to why, but it had become an erogenous zone in her mind. She fantasized about it frequently, wanting to touch it, to trace its perimeter and dip her tongue inside. *Oh, cripes, Jessica. Cut it out!*

Dragging her gaze from his navel, she glanced toward the groves. "The aroma is heavenly. And the scent seems even stronger at night."

"Amazing, isn't it? I think it has something to do with higher humidity and fewer exhaust fumes. Want to go for a walk through the groves?"

"I don't want to keep you from your workout."

"I'm not in any hurry. Come on." He put his hand to her waist and urged her along.

They walked across the lawn and into the edge of the groves, which began only a hundred feet or so from the house. As they strolled between the rows of lush trees, the fragrance grew even stronger and sweeter, and the white petals seemed to glow in the bright light of the full moon.

"Oh, this is glorious," she said, turning round and round as the scent tantalized her nose and washed over her skin like a perfumed vapor. "I love it. What kind of trees are these?'' She leaned closer to a flowering branch and inhaled deeply.

"Orange," he said, snapping off a stem of blossoms and threading it through her hair. "Navel oranges."

Her breath caught. She wasn't sure if it was the mention of "navel" or the feather-light touch of his thumb as it swept along her cheek that aroused her so. Or both. But an immediate sensual response tightened her belly and sent shivers racing over her body.

She couldn't move; she couldn't speak.

Was his thumb still on her cheek? Or was she feeling only an exquisite pattern lingering on her skin?

Their eyes met, and his were bright with reflected moonlight.

He lowered his face a fraction; she lifted hers.

Time was suspended for what seemed like aeons as the blossoms magically permeated the air, wafted into the space between them and spun an intoxicating web that drew them closer and closer until their lips touched.

That first tentative meeting of his mouth and hers set off an explosion. He pulled her hard against him, deepening the kiss and thrusting his tongue against hers. She moaned and pressed her body to his, slipping her arm around him, under his shirt, to splay her fingers across his broad back.

She ached to have her left hand free to explore the wonderful warm skin and taut expanse of his torso.

He cupped her buttocks and groaned against her

mouth with such a low, needful sound that she felt herself contract and go wet.

His mouth left hers and went to the vulnerable area of her throat. She tilted her chin to offer him more and writhed against the growing hardness she felt against her.

One of his hands moved under the cast that lay between them to find a breast, cover and stroke it, circle her nipple with his thumb. She sighed with pleasure. Awash with sensation, she ached for more intimate contact.

She wanted to strip off her shorts and his and feel him buried deep in her. "Oh, heaven help me!" she cried out in frustrated desire. She clutched at his waistband.

He froze. Then his hand withdrew slowly from her breast, and he stepped away. "I'm sorry, Jessica. God, I'm sorry. I didn't mean for that to happen. Did I hurt you?"

"Hurt me? Of course not. Why did you st—"

"Oh, hell," he said, turning away and raking a hand through his hair. "I've really made a mess of things now. Could you just forget that this ever happened?"

Talk about a bucket of cold water. Jessica suddenly felt like an idiot. "For sure. Consider it forgotten," she said flippantly. Head high and spine stiff, she wheeled and strode back to the house before she could burst into tears and embarrass herself further.

The magic of the night vanished.

Smells from the citrus blossoms turned cloying,

and she hurried inside and closed the door against their perfume. Unfortunately, she couldn't escape the imprint of Smith's mouth on hers, of his hands on her body. And the scent of the blooms, along with the scent of Smith, lingered on her clothes and in her mind. She hugged herself and shuddered.

What had happened? She should have asked, but she'd been too humiliated by his rejection to even consider it.

She replayed the scene over and over as she washed her face and dressed for bed, and for the life of her, she didn't understand what she'd done wrong. Something had turned him off. Maybe she'd merely been a disappointment to him. Oh, well. Her ego was bruised, but she'd survive. She supposed that they could simply be friends. Yes, that would probably be best.

When she left the bathroom and went to bed, her covers were turned down and a spray of orange blossoms lay on her pillow.

Now she was confused again.

Smith cursed himself for ten kinds of fool. What had possessed him to maul her like that? He thought he had better control. Obviously he hadn't. And her responsiveness almost had him stripping her and taking her under the trees. But he knew it wasn't him she was responding to; it was his twin brother. He realized that every time she looked at him, she saw Tom.

He couldn't abide the idea of being a stand-in for a dead man.

To escape his growing desire for her, he'd tried spending more time at the office, but there wasn't much for him to do there, and the days were boring. His grove managers had the farm under control. The old excitement for his work had disappeared, and grew worse after he'd lost the anchor of his family. The longtime relationship he'd had with Stephanie Bridges had even been a casualty of his increasing emotional disinterest, and his affairs since their breakup the year before last had been brief and impersonal.

For a long time, he'd been feeling unsettled and directionless—until Jessica had come along and turned his life upside down. She'd given him a brother and a birth mother. She had given him an identity and a new sense of purpose.

Now he couldn't imagine life without her. She filled his house with her vibrance and made the place come alive. He got a kick out of helping her get her business rolling, and her excitement over the contract with Neiman's spilled over onto him. God, she made him feel alive again, and she made him feel...

Horny.

Bitchin' horny.

Sweat rolled off him as he pumped iron.

The next three weeks were strange. Jessica stayed on a roller coaster of emotion, and Smith was the cause of the fluctuations. On the one hand, things were going fabulously for Jessica Miles bags. Smith had insisted on turning one of the guest suites on the south side of the house into a workshop and office for her. He'd even made a trip to Matamoros to pick up the beaded silk panels from Señora Lopez and deliver more packets of materials to her.

A count of her stock had produced only sixty-one finished evening bags stored in the RV. She shipped the fifty best to Dallas, and turned her attention to creating the rest, as well as replenishing her supply. Juanita Torres, Rosa's sister, was, indeed, an excellent seamstress, and Jessica hired Juanita along with two other women to make the bags under Jessica's supervision.

They were doing a great job with her designs. In fact, working only half days, the second fifty had already been completed with almost a week to spare—a good thing, since Sandi Meyers had called the day before with news. The first bags were a big hit with their customers, and several women had requested custom designs to go with particular gowns. Sandi had already ordered more, including a large number for Christmas sales.

Shirley had reported that orders for the back bag were coming in from their Web page and from the contacts Jessica had made during the past several months. Mack had his crew working overtime to fill the demand. Too, they had orders from a number of boutiques for additional evening bags.

Jessica was walking on air. She was ready to go to work full days, but Smith wouldn't hear of it.

"You still need to take it easy until Dr. Vargas gives the okay."

She'd wanted to argue, then thought better of it.

Her appointment with the doctor had been made for the following week. She could wait until then.

If things were going great professionally, they were less than perfect personally. Since that night in the groves when Smith had kissed her, he'd been downright cool to her. Not rude, simply reserved. He was always polite. Scrupulously, stiffly, maddeningly polite.

She would have been convinced that she imagined the passion of that night except that she'd caught him looking at her a few times with unmistakable lust in his eyes.

And then there was the horseback ride.

Jessica had been restless one afternoon, and she'd wandered down to the stables as she'd done several times. Dulce, Smith's paint mare, had become a friend, especially since Jessica often brought her a treat.

This time it was an apple.

"You'll spoil her." Smith stepped from the shadows of the stable.

"Only a little. She's such a sweetheart. Reminds me of Daisy in temperament. I miss her."

"What happened to her?"

"The horses were among the first things to go after Tom's accident. I just couldn't teach, take care of Tom and tend stock. Plus, they were a burden in other ways, and finances were tight." She rubbed Dulce's nose. "I wish I could ride her."

"I think that could be arranged." He started saddling the mare. When he finished, he led the paint out and climbed into the saddle. "Come on," he said, motioning her forward.

When she approached, he reached down and swept her up in front of him so that she sat sidesaddle with her right leg hooked around the horn and her left very close to him. "I meant to ride by myself. Can she handle double?"

"Sure, if we take it easy. And even though Dulce is very gentle, it's too dangerous for you to ride alone with your cast."

Jessica honestly couldn't remember if she enjoyed the ride or not. For the life of her, she couldn't have recalled the route they took. She was only aware of Smith's closeness, of the feel of his arms around her as he held the reins—and of the pounding of her heart. Every breath she took carried his scent. Heat seemed to radiate from him like an oven.

She became painfully aware of where her leg lay across the juncture of his. She wiggled.

He grabbed her leg. "Don't do that."

"Do what?" she asked, feigning innocence.

"Wiggle."

"Does it bother you?"

"It makes Dulce skittish."

He was lying, and she knew it. Her movements didn't make the mare skittish. It was Smith who was bothered. The sexual attraction between them was undeniable. Why wouldn't he admit it?

Maybe she was imagining Smith's interest in her, misinterpreting his smoldering stares, but that night at dinner it happened again.

Both casually dressed in shorts, they were eating outside by the pool as they did frequently. Jessica had glanced up from her iron-laden shrimp and oyster gumbo to discover him eyeing her with such unambiguous hunger that she felt like the main dish. By the time they got to dessert, she was squirming under his scrutiny.

Instead of looking away as she'd been in the habit of doing, a little devil on her shoulder urged her to challenge him. It was time that they were honest about this attraction between them.

She was weary of settling for erotic dreams; she was ready for the real thing.

Locking gazes with him, she picked up a strawberry with her fingers and leaned forward, her cast resting along the edge of the table and making a shelf for her breasts. She knew she had his attention when his eyes zeroed in on her cleavage. The air practically sizzled.

Very deliberately, she opened her mouth slightly and slowly drew the tip of her tongue over the strawberry.

She did it again.

He licked his lips.

She nipped a tiny bit of the berry, then licked her lips.

He swallowed.

She took another nibble as she kicked off her shoe. She slowly ran her toes up the inside of his leg.

His eyes widened.

Her toes slipped higher, and he dropped his fork.

Smiling, she held out the strawberry to him and,

her voice pitched low and laden with innuendo, said, "Want a bite?"

His molars must have been really grinding, because the muscles in his jaw twitched like mad.

"Tell me something," he said, his voice strangely hoarse.

"Anything."

"Did you love Tom very much?"

Jerking back her foot, she jumped up from her chair. "Damn you, Smith Rutledge," she shouted, throwing the strawberry at him. "Damn you to hell and back!"

Eight

Smith wouldn't even discuss the attraction between them. Mule-headed, he changed the subject whenever she tried to broach it. The only time he ever addressed the issue openly was when, totally frustrated, she asked him at breakfast one morning if he either had some dread disease or was impotent.

He'd almost choked on his corn flakes, then looked at her as if she had two heads. "Good God, no!"

If he wouldn't talk about the feelings between the two of them, his obsession with finding out more about Tom and Ruth Smith grew. He questioned her endlessly about them and about his grandmother Lula.

"If the doctor okays it for you to travel, I'd like to go to Oklahoma and see her."

"She won't understand who you are."

"Maybe not, but it's something I need to do. Will you go with me? Juanita can handle things while we're gone, don't you think?"

"Of course. She's great."

Smith also wanted to examine Tom's papers and the other few items of family memorabilia that she had boxed and stored in a shed at Shirley's house.

So, the following Tuesday, when her X rays and blood tests confirmed that everything was back to normal and her cast was sawed off, they made plans to go to Oklahoma. Smith even made an appointment to meet with Grandma Lula's doctor.

On Wednesday, they packed for an overnight stay and flew in the private jet to Bartlesville. Their relationship was back to strained: very polite on the surface; a steaming cauldron of sexual tension bubbling underneath. Jessica had decided to simply sit back and wait. Sooner or later Smith's ridiculous restraints were going to burst. *Then*, she thought, smiling smugly, *baby, look out.*

It was cloudy and cold when they landed in Oklahoma, and she shivered in her down jacket. Even though she wore slacks and boots, she was freezing by the time they got into the rental car. "I think my blood has thinned since I've been in the Valley. Or else I've gotten spoiled."

Smith turned the heater on high, then stripped off his leather jacket and made a blanket of it, tucking it around her legs. "Maybe that will help."

"Thank you."

"You're welcome."

All the politeness made her want to gag. "Now you'll be cold."

"Not likely. I'm hot-natured."

"Couldn't prove it by me."

"Dammit, Jessica, stop it! I can only take so much."

Shooting him a suggestive smile, she said, "Bet I can take a lot. Wanna try me?"

"That's enough, woman! I'm only human."

"No, *I'm* only human," she snapped. "I think you're trying to be a Vulcan."

"What's a Vulcan?"

She rolled her eyes. "Didn't you watch *Star Trek* growing up?"

"Oh, that kind of Vulcan. Sure I watched *Star Trek*. Every version and all the reruns. Did you like the first cast better than the second?"

Jeez, he was a slippery creature, she thought as he deftly turned the personal dialogue to impersonal chitchat. She let it go again. For now. At least he'd acknowledged—sort of—that he wanted more than friendship. His male instincts were giving him a fit. Good. Misery loves company.

The nursing home where Grandma Lula stayed was modest but clean and well run, and the old woman was neatly dressed when they arrived. She was also in her own world, withdrawn from reality. She addressed Jessica as both Ruth and Edwina, who had been an older sister, dead for twenty years or more. She didn't seem to recognize Smith, even to confuse him with Tom. She called him Frank once, but Jessica didn't know who Frank was.

Jessica knew that Smith was disappointed, but he was very gentle with the old woman, helping her open a gift that he'd brought her. She smiled at him when the box was opened and, in her only moment of lucidity, said, "Ohh, chocolate-covered cherries! My favorite."

They left soon after. Smith spoke with both the director of the nursing home and with Lula's doctor. He was willing to move her to the finest Alzheimer's facility in the country and foot the bill. Both the director and the doctor assured him that her care was excellent and that change might be more upsetting than helpful.

"I'm sorry that you couldn't really speak with Grandma Lula," Jessica said on their way to the hotel. "I know that you're disappointed."

"I am. But you warned me, so I didn't expect much."

"How on earth did you know that chocolate-covered cherries were her favorite? I'd forgotten that myself."

"I didn't know." He smiled. "But chocolate-covered cherries were my grandmother Beamon's favorite, and I took a chance."

They checked in at the hotel. Each of them had a minisuite, on the same floor but across the hall and a few doors down from one another. She cocked an eyebrow at him when she saw the arrangements.

He merely shrugged and tipped the bellman as he carried Jessica's overnighter inside her room. Smith grabbed his own bag. "I have to make some phone calls.'' He glanced at his watch. ''What time are we due at Shirley's?''

''About six.'' Shirley and Mack had invited them for a casual family dinner. ''It won't take more than fifteen minutes to get there, but maybe we should go early if you want to look through those boxes. She should be home from school by now. I'll call her.''

''Great.'' Smith hurried down the hall toward his suite. Or ''escaped'' might be a better description of his behavior.

Did he think that she was going to drag him into her room and have her way with him in front of the bellman?

She giggled. Now *there* was a thought. Rather than being put off by his avoidance of her, she was actually enjoying their little game. She thrived on challenge; she was a scrapper who went after what she wanted and hung in there—survival skills she'd learned as a kid. Was she stubborn? You bet. Admitting defeat had always been darned near impossible. That's why she'd stayed with Tom as long as she had.

The weather turned from bad to terrible. Rain, whipped by chill winds, poured down on them as they inched their way to the Mileses' house. The temperature hovered just above freezing. Smith had bought a golf umbrella in the hotel gift shop, and when they reached their destination, they huddled together under it and made a dash for the front door.

Shirley, a dark-haired gamin with an infectious

smile, met them with towels. She hugged Jessica, then turned to Smith.

Her smile died. "Dear God." Clearly stunned, Shirley tried to cover her reaction. "Come in. Come in. Let me take your umbrella. Isn't this rain awful? Mack's not home yet. He should be here any minute now."

Jessica had explained the relationship between Smith and Tom in her phone calls to Shirley, but she well understood the initial shock of seeing a man thought to be long dead. "Shirley, this is Smith Rutledge." She smiled. "It's amazing how much he and Tom look alike, isn't it?"

"Amazing doesn't cover it."

Gracious, Smith chuckled. "At least you didn't faint into your mashed potatoes. Shirley, I'm happy to finally meet you. Jessica talks about you and Mack all the time. And the kids."

"Where are the rug rats?" Jessica asked. "We brought presents."

"Upstairs, doing their homework," Shirley said. "They'll be down in a minute. May I get you something to drink?"

"I'd love a cup of coffee," Smith said.

"Me, too," Jessica added.

They both followed Shirley into the kitchen and sat on island bar stools, drinking coffee and chatting about business while Shirley slipped a casserole into the oven and prepared vegetables for salad.

Mack, a bear of a man with thinning sandy hair, soon joined them. After his initial shock seeing

Smith, they all settled into a comfortable conversation.

A few minutes later, Jessica suggested that she and Smith go look through the boxes stored in the shed out back. They took the umbrella and slogged through puddles to the storage shed.

The light was dim, and the space was crammed with not only Jessica's boxes but also with lawn mowers and water hoses and scores of assorted outdoor toys and cushions and gardening tools. It was soon evident that going through boxes in the cold, cramped conditions was impractical.

"Mark the ones you want to check," Smith said, "and I'll put them in the car before we leave. Or better yet, we can get them in the morning. The rain is supposed to clear tonight. We can take the boxes home with us and take our time sorting through them."

"Sounds good to me. My fingers are freezing and my nose is past numb. Is it still there?"

He laughed and rubbed her nose with the flat of his hand. "Let's go get you dry and warmed up."

Back inside, they shucked their wet shoes and toweled off again. Jessica borrowed a pair of Shirley's socks while Smith wore some of Mack's. Ricky and Megan, who were nine and seven, were thrilled over the computer games that Smith had brought them. The kids joined the grown-ups for dinner, eating quickly and begging to be excused to play the new games.

The adults lingered over dessert and coffee, enjoying an easy camaraderie despite the fact that Mack slipped and called Smith "Tom" twice.

Smith was good-natured about it. In fact, he encouraged Mack and Shirley to talk about Tom. After all, Mack had been Tom's best friend since they were boys.

Jessica and Shirley cleared the table, leaving Mack telling a story about a zany fishing trip that he and Tom had gone on as teenagers.

In the kitchen, Shirley stopped rinsing the plates and turned to Jessica. "Jess, be careful."

"About what?"

"About Smith. He's not Tom."

"I know that. They may look alike and have a lot in common, but in other ways, they're totally different. I admit that I had trouble at first, but after I was around him a while, I forgot about his looking like Tom. Now he's just Smith, not a look-alike. And he's a wonderful person. He's warm and confident and generous. All Smith's employees like him and respect him and are fiercely loyal. I think that proves that he's a genuinely nice guy. And he doesn't drink."

"Not like Tom."

"No, not like Tom," Jessica said. "Smith doesn't wrestle with the soul-deep demons that plagued Tom. He isn't weighed down with insecurities and bitterness so overwhelming that he makes life miserable for those around with his foul moods and terrible temper."

"In other words, it's as if someone took the old

flawed Tom and miraculously transformed him into a perfect new Tom?''

Shirley's comment hit Jessica like a wrecking ball.

"What are you saying?" Jessica asked quietly.

"I'm just asking you to be very careful. I don't want you to get hurt. When you love, you love with all your heart. I remember how much you loved Tom, and I remember the agony you went through in leaving him. And I also remember how awful that last year was for you. God knows, you deserve some happiness, but— Oh, I worry about you, you goose.''

Jessica hugged her friend. "I know you do, and I love you for caring, but there is no need to worry about me. I know what I'm doing, and I don't plan to do anything drastic.''

"How far has it gone?"

"How far has what gone?" Jessica asked, playing naive as she loaded silverware into the dishwasher.

"Don't give me that. There's enough electricity generated between the two of you to light up all Oklahoma and most of Texas. The man is nuts about you. A blind person could see it.''

"You think so?''

"I know so.''

"We haven't been to bed together, if that's what you mean.'' Jessica grinned. "But I'm working on it.''

Shirley sighed and shook her head, and the subject was dropped.

When the kitchen was clean, the women spent a few minutes going over business matters, including celebrating their profits and making arrangements for more fabric and findings to be sent to the Harlingen workshop.

Jessica didn't think about her conversation with Shirley again until she and Smith were on their way back to the hotel.

The old Tom transformed into a perfect new Tom? Did that explain her attraction to Smith?

Certainly Smith was far from perfect; she had no illusions about that. He had his own brand of demons about his past, but the concerns he contended with were light-years apart from the inner hell that bedeviled Tom. And he was stubborn. He and Tom had that in common. They wouldn't talk about the things that troubled them; they stuffed their feelings inside.

But maybe that was mostly a male thing. For years, she had begged Tom to talk with his doctor or see a therapist, but he refused. She went instead. The psychologist that Jessica had worked with had told her that women were much more likely to get help with their problems than men.

"I like your friends," Smith said, interrupting her thoughts.

"Thanks. They're nice folks. I'm sorry that we weren't able to go through the boxes tonight."

"No problem. I'm going over early in the morning, and Mack is going to help me load the ones we want to take with us."

They lapsed into a relaxed conversation, and the warm mood stayed with them until they reached Jessica's door at the hotel. Their good spirits turned awkward as Smith unlocked her door.

Jessica thought of a dozen things she could say or

do to make Smith squirm. Instead, she simply plucked the key card from his hand, said good-night and pecked him on the cheek. "See you in the morning," she said, smiling brightly and wiggling her fingers before she closed the door.

She turned the dead bolt and put on the chain, then peeked through the spy hole. Smith was still standing there.

His hand raked through his hair, then, after several seconds, he walked away.

Nine

Jessica and Smith sat in the middle of his den floor, boxes all around them. They'd been sorting through stuff for two hours. Some had been repacked; other items had been set aside to look through again. Still other things, like an old photograph album, had made him stop to examine them more carefully.

"Who's this?" he asked, pointing to a sullen, knobby-kneed girl and an older couple.

She smiled. "That's me with Mel and Leah Cutter, my foster parents. I must have been about nine."

"You don't look very happy."

Jessica laughed. "I wasn't. They were my third foster home in a year, and that picture was taken soon after I arrived. I came to love them dearly. They had two sons, both grown and living a distance away, and I think they missed having young people around. I became a combination daughter/granddaughter to them."

As he leafed through the album, she pointed out other family photographs in which she looked much happier. "This was my first Christmas with Mel and Leah, and this is my first bike." Other holidays were chronicled, as was a vacation to the Grand Canyon and another to Disneyland.

"Are they still living?"

"Leah died when I was eighteen, but Mel is still going strong. He moved to Florida to live with his oldest son the year after Tom and I married. I haven't seen him in about three years, but we talk on the phone fairly often. He's still quite a character." Looking wistful, she traced the features on a studio photograph of Mel tucked between the pages. "This was taken for the church directory the year before he moved. I miss him. And Leah."

"What about your birth parents?"

"I don't miss them. My father walked out when I was too young to remember, and my mother had a series of husbands and boyfriends after that. She cared more for men and booze than she did for me. The best thing that ever happened to me was when the agency took me from her. I rarely think of those days anymore. As I told you, Tom and I had a lot in common. I suppose my own desire to put my early childhood behind me was one of the reasons I never pressed him much about Ruth and their time together."

Other pages were filled with pictures of Jessica in

junior-high and high-school activities. She appeared lively and smiling in every photo—and cute as a button.

"You were a cheerleader, I see."

"Yep. For four years. And here is a picture of Tom and me dressed for my senior prom. Tom hated that tux."

Smith studied the image of his twin, young and awkward looking in an ill-fitting tuxedo. He smiled. "I can tell."

After Jessica's graduation pictures, the mounted photos stopped. A few loose ones were stuck in the back. "Leah got sick not long after I started college. She's the one who kept up with the album."

Sorting through another carton that Jessica identified as Grandma Lula's, Smith found a framed photograph of a teenage girl with long hair and sad eyes.

"That's Ruth," Jessica told him. "I think it was taken when she was about seventeen."

He stared at the picture for a long time, studying every part of his birth mother's face. He felt curiously empty. Her face was no more familiar to him than any stranger's would be, and he found no trace of family resemblance there. He set it aside carefully and probed deeper into the carton of keepsakes.

A heart-shaped box, its red satin cover stiff with age, yielded a handful of old snapshots and a thin packet of envelopes tied with a shoestring. The pictures turned out to be Lula and Malcolm Smith; the letters were from Malcolm to Lula. When he discovered what they were, Smith retied the letters, unread.

An old shoe box was filled with loose photographs, mostly school pictures of Ruth, and report cards and assorted mementos, including a blue-ribbon award and two red ones for unnamed feats.

"She was a good student," Jessica said, glancing through the report cards. "Especially in math. And according to this graduation program, she was salutatorian of her class."

"Here are her midsemester grades from the University of Oklahoma," Smith said.

"I never knew that she went to college."

"Looks like she was flunking."

"When was that? Early sixties? Maybe that's when she got involved with 'them hippies' that Grandma Lula always referred to."

"Probably." In the bottom of the carton, Smith found an old family Bible, large, black and worn. Carefully opening the musty pages, he found recorded there the birth and marriage and death dates of several relatives, beginning with Naomi Ruth Phillips, who was born May 5, 1899, and married July 21, 1916, to Samuel Elijah Thomas, born December 16, 1894.

"This must be Tom's great-grandmother and grandfather," Smith said. "And mine, too, I guess," he added, feeling as if he was finally beginning to fit pieces of a puzzle together. "Naomi and Samuel had three children. Edwina Althea, Lula Jane and Frank Warren Thomas. Frank died on December 7, 1941."

"The early days of World War II," Jessica said.

"Probably at Pearl Harbor. He was only nineteen. And here. Lula's husband, Malcolm, died in June of

1944. Tom's and my grandfather. I wonder if he died in the war, too?''

Two children were listed as born to Lula and Malcolm: a stillborn boy in August of 1941 and Ruth Anne Smith, born February 8, 1943. Edwina's marriage to James T. Patrick was listed, along with the birth of three daughters. No generations were listed after that.

''Do you know what happened to Edwina?'' Smith asked.

''She and her husband moved to California, and I seem to remember Tom saying that she died a long time ago. I think he and his grandmother rode the train to her funeral. As far as I know, they lost touch with Edwina's daughters.''

Smith flipped through the pages and found several yellowed newspaper clippings. Two were from the fifties, obituaries for Naomi and Samuel, another listed the death of Frank Thomas at Pearl Harbor. He also found the letter informing Lula of Sergeant Malcolm A. Smith's death in France.

In the very back, in the Book of Revelations, were three birth certificates. One was for a stillborn boy named Malcolm Alvin Smith Jr., another for Ruth Anne Smith, and the last for Thomas Edward Smith.

He looked at Tom's birth certificate for a long time, then rose and went to his study to dig out a copy of his own. When he laid them side by side on his desk, they were almost identical. Both babies had been born at the same hospital in St. Louis. Tom had been born four minutes before Smith and weighed six pounds, one ounce, considerably more than his own four pounds, two ounces. Tom's mother was listed as Ruth Anne Smith, father unknown, while the Rutledges were listed as Smith's parents.

Any lingering doubt that they were twins vanished. It was a certainty.

Pain ripped at his gut, and he wanted to bellow out his frustration.

Why? Why?

Why had his mother given him away?

Why had she kept Tom?

Why?

"Are you okay?" Jessica asked quietly, her hand stroking his back. He hadn't heard her enter the room.

He nodded. "I just have so damn many questions. Did Tom ever give you any clue that he knew about me?"

"No. I don't think that he did know. And he never talked much about his mother. Those years that he was with her were really bad."

"Dammit! Why didn't they take us both?"

"Who?"

"My folks. The Rutledges."

"Why don't you ask them, Smith? Don't shut yourself away from a family that loves you. Ask them the questions."

"I have. How can I get them to tell me why they didn't take Tom when they won't even admit that I'm adopted?" He cursed and slammed his fist on the desk.

Jessica leaned against his back and rubbed his shoulders. Before he even thought, he turned and took her into his arms. She rested her head against his chest and hugged him hard.

He squeezed her tight, laid his cheek on her soft mop of curls and held her. Just held her. With her there, he didn't feel so alone anymore.

It felt so good. So damn good.

The next day, Jessica realized that something about her wrist wasn't right. It was still weak and stiff. Trying to work with the evening bags only frustrated her. Smith insisted that she go back to the doctor. In fact, he not only drove her to the appointment, but he would have gone in the examining room with her had she not put her foot down.

Sometimes he hovered like a hen with a chick. It was exasperating, but at the same time a bit flattering. It was nice to be cosseted for a change.

Dr. Vargas didn't find a major problem. He referred her to a physical therapist, suggesting that a week or two of therapy and exercises was all that was needed. They went directly to the PT's office for evaluation and set up the first appointment for the following Monday.

"Oh, rats," Jessica said on the way home. "I'm sick of this. I'm ready to get back to normal."

"Not feeling a little sorry for yourself, are you?"

"Actually, I'm feeling a lot sorry for myself. We have tons of work to do, and I can't help."

"You help by supervising. You have to understand that your business is growing beyond the point that you can do everything yourself. You have to miss out on some of the fun of creating."

"Is that what happened to you?"

He nodded. "I got started making computers when I was in college. It was a kick. Then I started selling more and more of them, and the next thing I knew, I was employing a hundred people. It grew from there."

When they reached home, Juanita and the others had gone for the day. Jessica paced the workroom, restless. Her pacing continued through the house.

Smith found her staring out the window of the den, rubbing her arms.

"Are you cold?" he asked.

"No. I just feel antsy. And a little discouraged."

"Know what I think? I think you have cabin fever. You need a vacation."

"A vacation? I don't have time for a vacation. We have orders to fill and the Dallas Trade—"

"Whoa! You definitely need to kick back and have some fun. At least for the weekend. Ever been to South Padre Island?"

"No."

"Then let's go."

"Now?"

"Sure. It's only an hour's drive away, and I have a house there on the beach. Nothing soothes the nerves like listening to the sound of the ocean and watching the waves come in."

"My nerves are just fine."

He only grinned. "Go pack. Got a bathing suit?"

"No."

"We'll shop for one on the island."

* * *

Smith had said that South Padre was like another world—casual, relaxed. And it was true that her cares seemed to melt away as they drove over the long bridge to the narrow, sandy strip that guarded miles of the Texas coast.

"That's strange," she said.

"What?"

"The moment we started over the water, it was as if someone passed a magic wand over me and tension began to disappear."

Smith chuckled. "This place had that effect on me, too. I thought you might like it here. Before so many tourists found it, it was even better. Let's stop by one of the shops on the main drag and get you a bathing suit or two."

The main drag hosted an abundance of hotels, high-rise condos and all kinds of tourist shops and fast-food places. He wheeled into a parking place in front of a boutique displaying upscale sports clothes in their front window.

He went inside with her, and as she went through the bathing-suit rack from one end, he went through from the other, picking possibilities. Strangely, his choices were more modest than hers. His ran to one-piece suits while she tended to pick two-piece numbers that were wildly colored and considerably more revealing.

Jessica took six suits, three from his selections and three from hers, into the dressing room. After trying them all on, she settled on an electric-blue one-piece with high-cut legs and a flattering fit, as well as a hot-pink bikini that was beyond sinful. She considered modeling them for Smith's approval, then, smiling devilishly to herself, decided not to. She'd probably give him a coronary or he would insist on her wearing a T-shirt over them.

As it was, when she came out with the two she'd chosen, he and the saleswoman selected matching cover-ups for both. *And* a wide-brimmed hat. *And* matching swim shoes. *And* sandals.

"I don't need all this stuff," she whispered as the clerk went to find Jessica's size in the shoes. "It's much too expensive and totally foolish. I can use one of your old shirts as a cover-up, and who needs swim shoes, for goodness' sake? I may be in the black now with the Neiman's account, but I won't be for long if I start buying extravagant items like this."

"This is my treat," Smith said.

"Absolutely not. I'll pay for my own bathing suits—which are outrageous, by the way. I could have bought similar ones for a fourth the price at a discount store."

"Humor me here, Jessica. You're my guest. *I'll* pay for the suits." He held up a short robe that matched the bikini and a wraparound that went with the blue suit. "I kind of like these, and you might need them if the wind turns chilly. And you thought the hat was fun, so we'll get it. You'll need swim shoes on the beach." To the growing pile on the counter, he added a couple of other outfits he'd selected while she was in the dressing room, one a casual long knit dress and matching sweater, the other, knit pants and a fancy hooded sweatshirt. "We might want to go fishing."

She tried to argue, but Smith held firm. Rather than make a scene, she allowed him to pay. It wasn't as if he was hurting for cash, but she felt awkward letting him foot the bill for everything. And she wasn't likely to wear that long knit dress fishing.

After piling their purchases in the back seat, they drove north up the strip, then turned onto a parallel street along the beach where hotels and condos gave way to a series of beautiful beach houses on narrow lots. His was like a slice of sandcastle. Three-storied and with a turret, it was butter-yellow stucco with white trim and a sand-colored tile roof.

"Oh, I love it already," Jessica said as they waited for the garage door to go up.

As soon as he pulled the SUV inside, she hopped out and grabbed bags, eager to see the inside.

The interior was even more spectacular. "I love it. I love it," she said, awed by not only the beautifully furnished living/dining room but also by the view. The room, done mostly in rattan and with big, puffy couches, was a sumptuous turquoise and white with accents of purple and red. Colorful artwork filled the walls, but it was nothing compared to what she saw beyond the glass wall.

She dropped the bags and went immediately to the expanse of glass along the back of the room. Smith followed her, opening the door to the deck. A pool covered most of the small back enclosure, but her gaze went past the pool to the vast water beyond. Less than fifty yards away, white-capped waves rolled in, tumbling gently against the beach, washing the sand in immense irregular scallops.

"This is fabulous," Jessica said as she leaned against the wooden railing of the deck and stared out at the gulf. "Fabulous." She toed off her sneakers. "Let's go walk on the beach before it gets too dark."

Almost flying down the steps, she ran to the water's edge as if drawn by a wizard. Smith ran beside her. She felt like a kid, leaping and splashing along the flow of water against sand.

Standing in the path of waves, she wiggled her toes as water washed over her feet and laughed at nothing. "I love this! I love this! This is great."

Smith laughed with her. "I can see that you do."

After a half hour or so, when it had grown dark, they walked back toward the house. "If this were my place," she said, "I'd want to live here all the time."

"I usually stay here quite a bit. I like fishing or just taking one of the boats out."

"*Boats?* You have boats?"

"Yep. They're moored in Port Isabel just across the bridge on the mainland. I have one that I usually take out for deep-sea fishing, and I have a sailboat. Ever been sailing?"

"Never. I've always wanted to though. Movies I've seen make it look like fun. But it also looks like a lot of work, tending sails and hanging over the side to balance the boat. I don't know if I would be much help. I don't know one sail from another."

He laughed. "We won't be competing for the America's Cup tomorrow. I'll tend the sails, and I promise that you won't have to hang over the side.

We'll take the *Meg* out in the morning if this weather holds,'' he said.

''*Meg*?'' she asked, her eyebrows lifting. ''Named for an old flame?''

He smiled. ''Nope. Short for *Megabyte*. The big boat is the *Gigabyte*. You hungry?''

''I'm starved.''

''Me, too. There's a restaurant here that has the world's best snapper. They're known for their gumbo, too. You game?''

''Sounds good. But I'll need to change,'' she said, looking down at her wrinkled shorts and T-shirt.

''Not for South Padre. You might want to put on some shoes to protect your feet, but you look great as you are. Race you,'' he called suddenly, then sprinted for the house.

''Wait!'' she yelled, laughing and tearing after him. This was a whole new Smith.

Ten

"Look there," Smith said, pointing. "And there."

Jessica stood beside Smith at *Meg's* helm and marveled at the sight as they rounded the point. Dolphins arced from the water singly and in pairs, cavorting around the boat as they sailed from Laguna Madre toward the open waters of the Gulf. There must have been a dozen or more of the magnificent animals leaping and splashing, playing hide-and-seek among the gentle swells.

"They're like Flipper!"

Smith laughed. "I can't believe that you've never seen a dolphin in its native habitat."

"Believe it. Except in movies or on television, I've never seen a dolphin, period. Bartlesville isn't exactly near the coast, and I've never done much traveling.'' She held her face to the early-morning breeze, grateful for the warmth of the fancy sweat-shirt Smith had bought the day before. She hooked her arm through his and reveled in the intoxication of sight, sound and feeling. She drew in a deep breath of crisp, damp air filled with an amalgam of ocean smells. ''This is wonderful. I love sailing.''

Grinning, Smith steered around the rocky outcrop-ping. ''Goose, we're not even under full sail yet.''

''I don't care. I love it anyhow. It can only get better.''

And it did. Jessica delighted in the marvelous power of the boat as it skimmed across the water, relished the awesome engineless quiet that allowed them to hear the snap of sheets and the lap of water against the hull. Such a sense of serenity settled over her that Jessica was hard-pressed to even think of anything stressful.

The slight frown lines across Smith's forehead had relaxed when they'd crossed the bridge over the bay. They had smoothed out almost entirely since they'd been on the boat. He obviously found the island and the water as tranquilizing as she did.

Leaning back on one of the cushioned benches, she breathed a huge sigh. ''Now this,'' she said, ''is living. I could get used to this.'' But, she reminded herself, living like this all the time wasn't possible. She shoved the thought away. In another week, she'd be gone from the Valley. Concerns of the real world would intrude soon enough.

They sailed all morning, and only growling stom-achs drew them back to shore.

After lunch at the Yacht Club, they went back to the beach house and changed into swimsuits. She chose the blue one, and she could tell by the way his nostrils flared when he saw her in it that Smith hadn't anticipated the provocative fit. The legs were cut almost up to the waist; the back was indecently low and the neckline plunged nearly to her belly button. Wearing it required excellent posture.

Although he didn't say a word, he made a slight strangling sound as she sauntered across the living room. She tried to keep a straight face as she strolled past him, the cover-up draped casually across her arm. "Got a frog in your throat?" she asked innocently.

"No, no. Not at all." He grabbed the cover-up, which was little more than a large scarf, and draped it over her shoulders. "It might be a little chilly out. Wouldn't want you to catch cold."

Cavalierly, she tossed the wrap around her neck, aviator-style. "Think I should wear a coat?" A giggle escaped in a snort. Then another, until her shoulders were shaking with laughter.

Smith looked sheepish. "Are you sure that's one of the suits I picked out?"

"Positive. Don't you like it?" She pivoted slowly.

"It's...uh...a marvel of engineering."

"Is that supposed to be a compliment?"

"Oh, hell, Jessica. It's blue sin, and you look like a million bucks."

Slowly, she smiled. She suddenly felt like a million bucks. "Thanks. You don't look half-bad yourself, big guy."

He grabbed the scarf to pop her fanny, but she darted out of his reach and ran for the beach.

The sun had warmed the sand, and though the water was still too chilly to do much more than splash in the waves, it was a perfect day for splashing.

They frolicked like children in the water, then fell laughing onto towels in the sand.

Jessica rolled over onto her side facing Smith. Propping her head on one elbow, she said, "Thanks for bringing me here. I could live in this place forever."

"Somehow I knew you would enjoy the island."

"I can't believe that I've lived all my life and never knew I was a shore person. I'm going to head the RV to South Padre every chance I get."

"*Mi casa, su casa.* My house is your house. You're always welcome to stay here."

"Thanks. I may take you up on that."

He shut his eyes, and she took the opportunity to scrutinize him up close, to enjoy the sculpted shape of his tanned torso, the pecs, the abs. She studied the thin scar that ran the length of his sternum. When her finger traced the scar, his eyes popped open.

"What's this?" she asked.

"A surgery scar."

"What kind of surgery?"

"Heart."

"You've had *heart* surgery? You're not even forty yet."

"I had the surgery when I was two. I don't even remember it."

"What was wrong?"

"My dad could give you all the medical jargon, but, basically, I had a leaky chamber. Luckily, because my father was in the profession, I had the best pediatric cardiovascular surgeon in the country operate on me. Except for my mother hovering occasionally, I've never had any problems because of it. I played football and did anything else I wanted. I don't think about it anymore."

"Your father's a pediatric surgeon?"

"No. He's a heart specialist, but he deals only with adults. He was happy when my brother Kyle followed him into medicine, though Kyle's a plastic surgeon."

"Did you ever consider medicine?"

"Not for a minute. Blood makes me nervous. And I'd rather work on things that don't say ouch when I poke them."

She smiled. "Like computers and grapefruit?"

"Exactly. I don't think like Kyle or my dad. I've always liked to tinker, and I've always liked to grow things. I majored in agriculture in college. I guess I'm just a farmer at heart. In that way, I suppose Tom and I were more alike than Kyle and me."

"Tom did have a green thumb. We had a huge orchard, and his peaches were the best around. He loved our little farm. It broke my heart to have to sell it, but..." She shrugged.

"Why did you sell it?"

"Financial reasons." Jessica didn't want to go to that pity party again, so she quickly changed the subject. She wiggled her nose and patted it. "Is my nose red? It's beginning to feel a little funny."

He sprang up and looked at her face closely, frowning as he did so. "Oh, hell, Jessica. I forgot all about sunscreen. You're getting blistered. Let's get inside and put some aloe vera on you before you burn to a crisp."

They rinsed off sand and seawater at the outside shower, and Smith insisted on blotting her dry to prevent further irritation.

Once in the house, he led her to the kitchen, grabbed a pump bottle from a cabinet and squirted some thick aloe vera gel into her hand. "You cover your face," he said, "and I'll take care of your back."

"This feels great," she said, patting the balm over her nose and cheeks. "Goopy, but great."

"I should have remembered sunscreen. Sorry. Does it hurt?" he asked as he painstakingly smoothed aloe over her shoulders.

"Not really. And don't worry about it. I tan pretty easily. I think it's the little dab of Cherokee blood that I have."

"Cherokee? I'm part—" He stopped and gave a hollow laugh. "Well, since I'm not related to Grandpa Pete by blood, I guess I'm not part Cherokee after all."

"Actually, you are. I think Malcolm Smith was either half or a quarter. And I believe that Lula has some Indian blood, too. I'm not sure of the tribe. Just about everybody from Oklahoma has a little or a lot of Indian extraction. Most of us take pride in our heritage. Tell me about your grandfather."

"He's a character, and I've always idolized him.

All four of us grandsons are close to the same age, and we used to spend part of our summers at his place. Cherokee Pete is what everybody calls him, and he has long braids and a wicked sense of humor. Even though he has more money than Ross Perot, he wears jeans or overalls and runs a country store. He acts as common as shoe leather, but he has a library that is unbelievable, and he reads everything from John Grisham to Immanuel Kant.''

His big hands were marvelously gentle on her back and shoulders, spreading the aloe vera with feather-light strokes. They hesitated when they went to her thighs, but after a moment they moved on slowly down the back of her legs to her ankles.

Jessica couldn't help the sigh that escaped her lips. His touch was bone-melting. Cool gel, warm skin, delicious enticement of mind and body. ''I'd love to meet him sometime.''

''If you ever go through East Texas, drop by. He'll feed you some of his famous chili and show you his pet rattlesnake. Turn around,'' Smith said quietly, his voice hoarse.

She turned.

He knelt on the floor, the pump bottle beside him. He didn't look up. Instead, he dispensed gel into his palm, rubbed his hands together and started his slow stroking with the tops of her feet. Standing immobile while his hands spread such glorious pleasure over her skin was one of the most seductive experiences of her life.

By the time he reached her knees, they were quivering.

Still, he didn't look up.

Filling his palms again with aloe, he slid his hands leisurely up the front of her thighs, his thumbs grazing the inner, sensitive areas. She sucked in a gasp and grabbed his shoulders for support.

He kept his head down. For what seemed like aeons, his hands stayed there, fingers resting at the edge of the high-cut leg of her suit, thumbs a millimeter below the hem of the crotch.

Desire rolled over her in waves. Her fingers dug into his shoulders. "Smith?" she whispered.

"Shh. Don't say anything. Just give me a minute." He took a deep, shuddering breath, then moved his hands and stood. He handed her the bottle. "Can you get the rest?" he asked, still not looking at her.

She licked her lips and sucked in a shuddering breath of her own. "No. I'd rather you do it."

He held out his hand. She squirted gel into it. Starting with her fingertips, he covered first one arm, then the other.

Her heart pounded in anticipation. The heat that rose from her had nothing to do with the sun.

He took one last measure of aloe, rubbed his palms together, then stared at her chest for the longest time. Slowly he moved. His hands cupped her throat, then slid slowly down and out over her collarbone, traveling to the shoulder straps of her suit, stopping, then easing the straps aside with the edges of his little fingers. The heels of his hands skimmed the swell of her breasts as they moved in a sensuous glide back toward the center of her chest. Careful not to go beyond the boundary of the fabric, his fingertips slowly stroked the skin revealed by her plunging neckline.

For the first time, he lifted his head and looked at her.

His eyes had gone dark. His jaw was clenched. An expression of raging hunger etched his face.

Her belly contracted; her yearnings ran rampant. A low throb ached so awfully that it almost overwhelmed her. The bottle of aloe vera she gripped dropped to the floor.

His fingers lingered between her breasts. "Jessica," he said in a ragged whisper, "this is killing me. Tell me to stop."

"Don't stop." Her gaze locked with his. "Please, don't stop."

His hands moved inside the blue fabric to cup and free her breasts. His eyes left hers to look down. "Beautiful," he whispered. "Beautiful. I want a taste. Just one taste."

He bent to circle one nipple with his tongue, then take it into his mouth and suck gently. Jessica nearly went out of her mind. She grabbed handfuls of his wiry hair and pulled him closer, rubbing her breast hard against his mouth, straining for more of the glorious sensation.

Smith groaned and stripped off her bathing suit in one swift motion. His gaze feasted on her. "Damn, you can't imagine how often I've lain awake at night wanting to do that, wanting to strip you naked. And wanting to do this," he said, kneeling in front of her, burying his face against her pubis and stroking her buttocks and hips. "And damn me to hell, a taste won't do it. I want all of you."

"I want you, too." She lifted his face. "Now, Smith. Please. I'm dying."

He stood, swept her into his arms and strode to his bedroom. As soon as he laid her down, he stripped off his swimsuit and reached for a condom. He was spectacularly tumescent, and she watched wantonly as he rolled on protection, then turned to her.

"I'll make it better for you next time, love. I swear I will, but I can't wait much longer. I've ached for you too long."

"I don't want you to wait," she said, opening to him, reaching for him. "I'm as ready as you are."

Kneeling between her legs, he lifted her hips and licked her. She almost came off the bed.

"You're wet. Hot and wet. God, I could eat you up."

"I want you inside me. Now. Hurry."

Coming to her swiftly, he covered her mouth with his and plunged deeply, his tongue driving as hard and deep as his shaft.

She gasped as spasms gripped her almost immediately. Awash with pleasure, her back bowed, she wrapped her legs around him, pulling him deeper, heightening her sensation and wringing a cry from the depths of her being. Her climax went on and on and on, convulsing her body and detonating an explosive ejaculation from him.

"Oh, Jessica, love. Oh, Jess," he said over and

over as his body shuddered so violently that the bed shook. Dropping kisses over her face, he called her name again and again. "Damn Tom! Damn him to hell for having you first!"

Eleven

Stunned by Smith's words, Jessica went dead still. "Why did you say that?"

He rolled to his back and flung his forearm over his eyes. "Oh, hell, Jessica, I'm not a fool. I know that every time you look at me you see Tom—alive and well again."

She turned on her side and slid her hand up his chest. "You're wrong. I know the difference, believe me, I do. Tom is gone. I realize that. I put the past behind me a long time ago. You're a very unique man, Smith, and it was *you* that I wanted, *you* that I made love with." She touched her tongue to his nipple, then laid her head on his chest and snuggled close. "No man has ever had the effect on me that you do. *No man.*"

He gathered her to him. "I'd like to believe that."

"You can take it to the bank, mister. Until I met you, I'd always considered myself rather...sexually sedate. Now it seems all I can think of is getting into your pants."

He laughed. "Make that two of us. I haven't had a decent night's sleep since you showed up in the cafeteria."

"What is it? Pheromones, you think?"

Rolling her over, he said, "It might be your beautiful eyes." He kissed each eyelid. "Or your sexy mouth and killer smile." He kissed her lips. "Or this little dimple." He kissed her chin. "Or it may be this cute butt that keeps me horny." He caressed her bottom. "Or these." He cupped a breast and flicked a nipple with his tongue. "Oh, babe, I have heavy dreams about these. Or maybe it's just the whole package."

There wasn't an inch of her that he didn't kiss and caress and croon over. She was a mindless blob long before he'd visited every site with his mouth and his hands. She'd never been made love to the way that he made love to her, as if she were a goddess to be worshiped. Heady stuff. Feeling like the most desirable woman in the world freed her from inhibitions, gave her power to take the initiative and explore new pleasures with his body.

He seemed to love everything she did. And when they came together again, it was with such a sense of rightness that she wept with the volatile response he wrung from her innermost core.

He had demanded, and she had given, her all.

Nothing was held back. Her body rocked with a second climax as potent as the first. A powerful new emotion washed over her and tears sprang to her eyes.

"Jess, darlin', why are you crying?"

"I—I think I love you."

He laughed and hugged her close. "Oh, babe, I hope so. God, I hope so."

They napped and made love the rest of the afternoon, then showered together and made love again. Smith insisted on toweling off Jessica and blow-drying her hair. He enjoyed every minute of it. He hadn't felt so good in years.

"Are you sure that you know what you're doing?" she asked as he wielded the brush and dryer. "My hair is a curly mop that's impossible to manage."

"Trust me, darlin'. My hair wasn't always this short. When I was a kid, long hair was the in thing, and I looked like I was wearing a red fright wig until my mom taught me how to handle it. Talk about a curly mop, I've got one, and it's like steel wool. I love your hair, the color, the texture, and the way it coils around my fingers. It's as soft and fine as spring cornsilk."

She laughed. God, how he loved that laugh. "What a lovely bunch of blarney. That must be the Irish in you talking."

"Irish?"

"You look Irish to me. I always figured that your father..." She shrugged.

"Could be. It's a shame that there's no way to

find out." Determined not to get into the relatives question, he gave Jessica's hair a final fluff and turned off the dryer. Turning her to the mirror, he said, "Well, what do you think?"

"It's...big." She giggled. "I think I look like a cross between a blond Diana Ross and a Chia Pet."

"I think it looks sexy. I like it loose and all..."

"Frizzy?"

"No. All I can think of is having that glorious hair spread out over my pillow. I don't know why you always wear it in a pigtail—not that your pigtail doesn't look great—"

She rose and tiptoed to peck his cheek. "Stop while you're ahead, big guy. I'll see if I can tame it a little and still wear it down. I'm hungry. How about a peanut butter sandwich?"

"How about coconut shrimp in peanut butter sauce? Put on that new dress we bought, and I'll take you dining and dancing."

"*Dancing?* Do you dance?"

"Is the pope Catholic? Honey, I'm a dancing fool. My mama and her sister made all their boys learn to dance and appreciate the finer things in life. I can waltz, I can fox-trot, I can two-step. Hell, sugar, I can even tango and cha-cha—not to mention all those low-down, belly-rubbing moves."

He grabbed her and did a few steps to prove it. But she lost her towel, and he forgot about dancing. All he could think about was the swell of her breasts as they pressed against his chest and the softness of her skin under his hands.

"I love to dance, but I haven't been in years, not

since high-school days. I don't know if I even re-member how.''

He looked up from the shoulder he was nibbling. ''Tom didn't take you?''

''He didn't care much for it.''

''That's where we're different for sure. Don't worry, it'll come back to you. Paint your toenails red, woman, and put on your dancing shoes. We're gonna boogie tonight.'' He went back to his nibbling. ''Um, uh, later.'' His hands cupped her butt, and he licked a path up her neck.

She laughed again and eased from his grip. ''Oh no you don't. You have to feed me first. *And* take me dancing.'' Rewrapping the towel around her, she scooted out of his bathroom. ''Get your clothes on,'' she called over her shoulder. ''I'll be ready in fifteen minutes.''

As he watched her leave, he could feel himself grinning like a cow eatin' cabbage, as Grandpa Pete used to say. God, he felt great. Like somebody had turned a light on inside him and flooded all the dark places. He was crazy about Jessica. Totally nuts about her. If only—

No. Hell, no. He wasn't going there. Not now. Dammit, he was going to enjoy this weekend. For a couple of days, he was going to pretend that a guy named Tom never existed. Or at least he was going to try his damnedest to.

Whistling, he went to his closet.

Jessica didn't have any red polish, but she found a bottle of very bright pink in the vanity drawer. She tried not to think of who it might have belonged to. Instead, she hummed as she brushed her toenails with it.

The sleeveless knit dress, powder blue with a white fish design, was a perfect fit. It came almost to her ankles and had a side slit to the knee. Her nose was still a little reddish, but not neon, and a dab of foundation covered that. She didn't need blush, only a bit of lipstick and mascara. She added silver earrings, then tackled her hair.

Actually, it didn't seem too bad—if you didn't mind the I-just-got-out-of-bed look. She brushed back the sides and secured them with a clip at the crown, letting a few strands escape around her face. She really needed a good haircut now that she could afford it.

A touch of perfume to pulse points, and she was ready. She picked up her jacket and checked her watch. Oops. She had taken twenty minutes instead of fifteen. Then she looked down at her feet and wiggled her bare, pink-tipped toes. Shoes. She needed shoes.

The white sandals Smith had insisted on buying were perfect.

Now she was ready.

When she opened her bedroom door, Smith was waiting. Wearing a leaf-green sport shirt and khakis, he was handsome as buttered sin, and the light that shone from his eyes when he spotted her made her go warm all over.

He gave a wolf whistle. "Dynamite, darlin'."

She held up one foot and wiggled her toes. "I couldn't find any red polish. Will pink do?"

"Pink is perfect."

"I'll bet you say that to all your lady friends." She laced her arm through his.

"I don't have any lady friends. Haven't in a long time."

Jessica suddenly felt very smug, but she tried not to grin. She didn't succeed.

Jessica sighed and snuggled against Smith as the disc jockey played a slow ballad. The coconut shrimp had been scrumptious, the turtle cheesecake totally sinful, and Smith was a fabulous dancer. In the past hour, they'd done everything but the cha-cha and the tango, and she'd had a blast.

"I haven't danced this much since I was seventeen years old," she'd told him. "I'd forgotten how much I love it."

"A shame. You're a natural."

And he'd been right. All the moves had come back to her, and the steps she didn't know, she'd learned quickly from Smith's strong lead, laughing as he whipped her around in a country swing or a lively two-step. He was sexy as all get out with his loose-hipped style, and she hadn't missed the blatant perusals by a couple of single women in the room. She'd had the childish urge to say something really obscene to them or pin a sign on his back saying, He's Mine!

All evening they'd had the small dance floor of the hotel bar practically to themselves. Only one or two other couples joined them occasionally. The smattering of other patrons had drinks at the bar or in a dark corner of the room, and they soon thinned out, leaving them alone except for the disc jockey and the bartender. Smith had tipped the employees generously, and they seemed willing to stay open for as long as necessary.

"Getting tired?" he asked.

"A little. But I don't want the evening to end. I'm having a wonderful time. Besides, we haven't done the cha-cha yet."

He grinned. "I doubt that this guy has a cha-cha in his repertoire. I'll ask. Want something to drink while I check?"

"I'd love another ginger ale."

He seated her at the table, held up two fingers to the bartender, then went to speak with the disc jockey.

He returned a few minutes later with news. "We're out of luck on the cha-cha, but he thinks he might have something with a Latin beat. He's checking while we take a break."

As it turned out, the closest thing he had to a Latin beat was some old Jimmy Buffett. They danced to that, then decided to call it a night.

"I think I have some tango music at the house," he whispered as he nibbled her ear. "We can get naked and dance in the kitchen."

"Smith!" she said in mock outrage, then giggled and hurried to the car.

Dancing naked in the kitchen was a totally new experience, but they did it—and she loved it. They did lots of things that night that she'd never done before, and she enjoyed all of them.

It was glorious to be able to say or do anything she wanted without censoring it first. She was giddy with the freedom of it.

And the next morning they went out on the boat again. She was becoming quite a sailor, she discovered. She especially liked making love on the deck. Smith was very careful to cover her exposed parts with sunscreen, and the application had been some very hot foreplay. In fact, some of the spots he'd insisted on attending to would never see the light of day.

The weather was warm and perfect, and there wasn't a soul in sight, so they sailed for an hour or more without a stitch on. It was sensational.

"This is a kick," she said as she stood in front of Smith at the helm, her hands on the wheel, his on her. "I can't believe that I'm doing this."

"Me neither."

"You haven't done this before?"

"Nope. It never occurred to me before. Until I met you, I'd never thought of doing a lot of things I've done with you. You inspire me."

His left hand stroked her breasts while his right slipped between her legs. She lay back against him as he kissed her neck and shoulder and stimulated her with his fingers.

Moaning with pleasure, she gripped the wheel tighter. "I'm going to capsize us if you keep that up."

"I'll save you. Let go, darlin'. Enjoy it."

She did.

Then they switched places.

She felt completely shameless. It was wonderful.

"I'll bet that helicopter got an eyeful," Smith said.

"*Helicopter?*" Jessica squealed, automatically looking up and trying to cover herself.

He started laughing.

Only a few puffy clouds and a lone bird were visible in the sky. "You stinker!" She popped his bottom. "You scared me half to death."

Still laughing, he gathered her into his arms. "Sorry, darlin', but around you, I feel like a kid again."

She snuggled close and smiled. "I know the feeling. Walking into that cafeteria in Harlingen was the luckiest thing that ever happened to me in my entire life. I love you so much."

That night as they lay together in bed, a hard knot began to form in Smith's chest. Jessica slept in his arms, and the waves washed against the shore with the rhythmic sound that always put him right to sleep. Sexually sated—hell, sexually exhausted—he should have been out like a light.

But he wasn't. He was wide awake.

Thinking about Tom.

And Jessica. Tom's wife.

Smith had been handed everything—wealth, education, a loving family, boundless opportunities. Grandpa Pete had given him a million dollars' seed money when he graduated from college. He'd doubled that amount in no time, and his grandfather had given him an extra ten million in the same deal he had with all his grandchildren.

Everything Smith touched turned to gold, his business prospered, he built his dream homes, and he could have any woman he wanted. Life had been a ball until he'd found out he wasn't the Rutledges' son. That had been sobering, a hell of a lick, but it was nothing compared to what Tom had endured.

His other half had lived a hardscrabble existence with a drug-addicted mother and a cold grandmother, had to settle for taking a few junior-college courses at night while he busted his butt for peanuts. Tom had only had a few pleasures in life, a paltry few things to give him comfort and pride: his small business, his farm and his wife.

Fate had dealt him another cruel blow when he had that accident that left him paralyzed. Not only couldn't he walk through his orchards anymore or ride his horse, he had to watch the farm being sold to pay his bills, watch his business go down the tubes because he couldn't work anymore.

And his wife. Jessica.

She was bound to have been the real light of his life. Tom had died and lost even her. Lost her and left her with staggering medical bills.

And now, instead of honoring his twin's memory by merely helping his widow, Smith had taken her into his bed. None of it was Jessica's fault. He felt, despite anything she said, that, unconsciously at least, he was a stand-in for Tom. Smith had stolen even that from his brother.

He tried to rationalize away his feelings, tried a dozen approaches. He was an intelligent man; he'd read a little psychology. But none of the approaches he tried worked.

Guilt clawed at his belly.

Twelve

The smell of coffee teased Jessica awake. As had quickly become a habit, she reached for Smith. The place beside her was empty. She stretched and rose, looking around the room for something to put on. Lord only knew where her clothes were. She pulled on one of Smith's T-shirts and went looking for him.

He was in the kitchen, just slipping a pan of biscuits into the oven. "Good morning, sleepyhead," he said when he spotted her. "I was about to wake you. It's time to return to civilization." He picked up an egg and cracked it into a bowl. "How do you want your eggs? Scrambled or scrambled?"

Still drowsy, she came up behind him, wrapped her arms around his waist and pressed her cheek against his back. "I want them later. I need coffee first. Do we have to go back?"

"''Fraid so, Cinderella. You have a business to run. I have a business to run. And you have a physical-therapy appointment this afternoon.''

"I don't think I even need physical therapy anymore. I'm using my hand and wrist much better. See?" She slid her hands down his fly.

"Whoa, there," he said, capturing her fingers. "If you start that, our biscuits will burn, and I'll be late for my meeting. Why don't you grab a cup of coffee and take a quick shower? By the time you're dressed, I'll have our food ready."

A bit puzzled by his attitude, she got a cup of coffee and retreated to her room. Since when did Smith care more about biscuits burning than making love with her? She shrugged. He mentioned a meeting. Maybe he had his mind on a sticky situation at the company.

She showered, dressed and quickly tossed her things into her overnighter, putting the overflow into the shopping bag from the boutique. Smith was just dishing up eggs when she returned.

"Mmm, this looks scrumptious," she said. "I didn't know you could cook." She wrapped her arms around him and started to give him a kiss.

"Careful," he said, lifting the frying pan over her head and easing away. "I don't want to burn you. Sure I can cook—as long as it's canned biscuits and scrambled eggs. I can also open a decent can of chili." He grinned. "Sit down and dig in. I'll get the jelly. Grape or strawberry?"

"Surprise me."

He brought both.

They ate at the table overlooking the water, and she longed to be going out on the boat instead of returning to Harlingen. "How can you bear to leave this place?"

"Sometimes it's hard, but I remind myself that even paradise gets boring after a while. I appreciate it more the next time I come back."

"Maybe we can come back next weekend."

"You have to leave for Dallas, remember? The trade show is next week."

"Oh, rats," she said, "you're right, and I have a million things to do to get ready. Are you going to Dallas with me?"

"Babe, I wish I could, but I've been letting a lot of things slide at the office, and my desk is piled up. I've got an important board meeting coming up, and I have enough conferences scheduled to choke a horse."

"Oh," she said, feeling suddenly guilty. She was the reason that he'd been neglecting his work. Since she'd been in town, he'd spent very little time at his office. Corporations the size of his didn't run themselves. "Well, let's get this show on the road." She grabbed his plate. "I'm packed. Get your stuff together while I wash the dishes."

"You're on, but just stack them in the sink. The maid will be here soon, and she'll clean everything."

If Jessica had seen Smith's mood lighten when they crossed the bridge to South Padre, the reverse was true on the way home. The closer they got to Harlingen, the quieter he got. She could hardly pull two words from him. Oh, he was polite. Smith was always polite. But he was becoming...aloof.

And his frown lines were back.

And he got stopped for speeding.

As it turned out, he knew the officer and got off with a warning, but he seemed in a prodigious hurry to get back home. When she mentioned his unusual haste, he said, "When I have things on my mind, my foot tends to get a little heavy. Sorry."

"Anything I can help with?"

"No."

When they reached his house, he grabbed their luggage while she carried the shopping bag. She had assumed that he might take her bag to his room, but he didn't. He set it inside the door to her room. Honestly, she felt a little hurt. She started to mention it, but she didn't feel as uninhibited with him as she'd felt yesterday. Barriers had gone up between them, subtle barriers perhaps, but definite barriers.

"If you'll excuse me, I need to change and get going." He checked his watch. "I'll probably be tied up most of the day. Ric will drive you to the therapist this afternoon."

"I don't need Ric to drive me. I can drive myself if you don't mind my borrowing one of your cars. Or I can rent one. That's what I usually do when I'm in an area where I need to be mobile. The RV isn't the most practical vehicle for zipping around in."

"Hell, you don't need to rent a car," he said sharply. "I've got a garage full. Pick any one you want. The BMW might be the easiest to maneuver. The keys to all the vehicles are by the back door."

He checked his watch again. "Anything else you need?"

Stunned by his change in attitude, she simply stared at him in bewilderment. She suddenly felt like a monumental bother. "No," she finally said. "Not a thing."

He took off down the hall like his tail was on fire.

"Talk about Jekyll and Hyde," she muttered. Maybe he was more like Tom than she'd first thought. Tom had always been a little distant, but she'd invariably been able to tell when one of his black moods set in. He would become short with her, then more and more withdrawn. She'd learned to leave him alone and give him a wide berth. Confrontation was the worst thing she could do. Maybe Smith was the same way.

The notion troubled her.

No, she couldn't believe that Smith was like Tom. Something was bothering him. Business probably. Or PMS. She giggled as she unpacked.

A few minutes later, she went to the workroom. Juanita and the others were already there and busy. She soon lost herself in tasks, and before she knew it, it was lunchtime. The seamstresses left for the day, and Jessica stayed to sketch a new Christmas design.

She didn't get much done. She kept finding herself staring out the window, remembering the glide of the sailboat, the feel of wind in her hair, and Smith's hands on her body.

"Miss Jessica?"

She glanced up to find Rosa with a tray in her hands. "You need to eat your lunch."

"Oh, thanks, Rosa. I think I'll eat by the pool."

She started to take the tray, but Rosa said, "I'll carry."

"My wrist is fine now. I can manage."

"Mr. Smith said I should take very good care of it. I'll carry."

Lunch by the pool alone wasn't the same. She ate quickly and went to get ready for her therapy appointment.

The house seemed very quiet when Jessica returned. Only Rosa was there, shelling peas for dinner. She tried to help, but Rosa shooed her from the kitchen.

She tried to work, but she felt too restless. And it was too early to phone Shirley or any of her other friends; they were all still at work.

Mel. She hadn't talked to him in ages. Buoyed by the prospect of a long conversation with her foster father, she phoned Florida.

Mel was at the senior citizens center, his daughter-in-law told her. Playing dominoes with his cronies. He would be sorry to have missed her call. Jessica promised to call again later in the evening.

Feeling very alone, she strolled through the groves, noting the tiny fruit forming on the trees now that the buds had gone. She wandered down to the stables. Rio barely paid her any attention, but Dulce, the paint mare, whickered when Jessica neared.

"Hello there, girl," she said, giving her a pat. "Sorry I didn't bring you a treat. I just came to talk. Are you game?"

Dulce tossed her head as if she knew what Jessica was saying. She laughed and gave the horse another pat. Picking up a brush, she began to groom the mare, talking to her about this and that, mostly about Smith and the conflicting messages she was getting from him. "Men are strange sometimes, aren't they?"

Dulce flicked her tail and looked at Jessica with big brown eyes that almost said, "Ain't it the truth."

After half an hour or so, Jessica tossed the brush aside. "Thanks, Dulce. I feel much better now. We'll have to talk again."

It was almost dinnertime when she returned to the house. Rosa met her. "Ah, there you are, Miss Jessica. Mr. Smith called. He said that he couldn't get home for dinner tonight, and you should eat without him. Ricardo will serve anytime you're ready."

"Thanks, Rosa. Just let me wash up."

Although she'd eaten alone for ages, Jessica found that she'd grown used to company. Smith's company. The food tasted like cardboard.

Not only did Smith not make it home for dinner, he was still out when she dressed for bed. She lay awake for the longest time, listening for him to come in. She fell asleep sometime after midnight, then awoke about one-thirty when she thought she heard him.

Quiet footsteps stopped outside her door, then moved on down the hall.

The next morning he was gone before breakfast.

That night he didn't come home for dinner again. He relayed messages to her through Rosa.

"He's working very hard," Rosa said. "Problems with the company and big meetings."

Maybe so, Jessica thought, shrugging. But he could at least call me, or come in to kiss me good-night. If he was tired, she wouldn't make any demands on him.

Or maybe this was Smith's way of giving her the brush-off. Maybe the intimacies they'd shared over the weekend meant more to her than him. She wasn't sophisticated in the intricacies of affairs. She didn't know all the rules. Tom was the only other man she'd ever made love with, and their sex life had been rather...perfunctory. And when his drinking had gotten worse, it became almost nonexistent.

Smith was light-years beyond her in technique and experience. Were the things he'd said to her just a line? Had their time at South Padre been merely casual sex to him? She was very confused. And hurt.

She wanted to think that he was simply preoccupied with business; she wanted to give him the benefit of the doubt. But no way was she going to get into another relationship with a man who kept her emotionally wrung out and made her question her self-worth. Tomorrow, she planned to confront Smith about her feelings. And if he didn't give the right answers, she was out of there. She'd pack up her RV and hit the road.

That night she fell asleep hugging her pillow and feeling determined.

Sometime during the night she awoke with a figure standing over her. "Smith?" Still half-asleep, she automatically held out her arms to him.

He took one of her hands between his and patted it. "Sorry. I didn't mean to wake you, Jess. Go back to sleep."

Before she could respond, he was gone.

She sat up and looked at the red numbers on the clock. Two-eighteen.

What was that all about? She was wide-awake. And her stomach was in a dozen knots.

"Enough of this crap!" She threw back the covers and stalked to Smith's door. First she knocked. When there was no answer, she threw open the door and strode into his room. He wasn't there, but she could hear the shower running.

Charging in that direction, she muttered to herself as she went. She meant to have it out with him now, tonight. In the bathroom, she flung open the shower door.

Wet and stunned, Smith simply stared at her for a moment. He was fully aroused. Seeing him set off an immediate sexual response in her, one so titillating that the urgency of her mission went completely out of her head. *No need to waste it,* she thought with impish glee as she stripped off her gown and tossed it aside.

When she started to step into the shower, he said, "Wait! Don't get in here."

"Why not?"

"Because you'll freeze your butt off." He hurriedly turned off the water, got out and grabbed for a towel.

She stepped between him and the towel rack. "We

need to talk." She put her arms around him and pressed herself against his body. "You're cold."

"No," he said. "I'm not. That's the problem. It's late. Why don't we talk in the morning?"

"Because you'll be off in another meeting. I want to talk now. Well...maybe in a few minutes. Who are you so hot for?" She rubbed seductively against him.

"Oh, Jess," he groaned. "Don't do that, babe."

She did it again. "Tell me who you're so hot for."

His mouth covered hers with a hunger so powerful that her knees gave out. When he came up for air, he clutched her to him. "You, dammit. It's you I stay hot for. It's killing me, Jess. God help me, I can't keep you off my mind." He lifted her and strode to his bed.

Then they both went wild.

Jessica woke at seven-thirty in Smith's bed. Alone. He was gone again, and they hadn't talked much at all—certainly not about why he'd been avoiding her. And it was plain to her that he had been.

Sighing, she rose, found her gown and hurried back to her room to dress. Before this day was out, she was determined that she was going to have a powwow with Smith. Obviously the problem wasn't that he was tired of her. He hadn't seemed to be able to get enough of her. But something was wrong. Very wrong. She didn't buy the meetings story.

Doing her best to push the problem aside, she and the seamstresses worked all morning. She boxed the last of Neiman's order for shipment and selected the samples she would be using at the trade show. When all the samples were sealed in their cartons, she said goodbye to the women, hugging each one and thanking them for their excellent help. She'd also added a bonus in their pay envelopes. All the orders for Jessica Miles evening bags had been filled ahead of time, and this was the last day they would be working until she returned from Dallas.

Feeling very proud of her accomplishment, she went to lunch with a spring in her step and a goofy smile on her face. Rosa had another message for her.

"Mr. Smith won't be home for dinner."

The announcement was a downpour on her parade. Blast it! She was tired of this game. "Then I won't be, either."

After her physical-therapy session, she got her hair trimmed and shaped at a salon her therapist recommended. She even got a manicure and a pedicure. She had her toenails painted red.

She went shopping at the mall, ate dinner at a Chinese place there and went to a movie. It was almost ten o'clock when she got home.

Smith was waiting at the door. "Where the hell have you been?"

She blinked. "I beg your pardon?"

"Where the hell have you been?" His eyes blazed, and she could practically see smoke coming from his ears.

"Out."

"Out where?" he demanded.

"I had *meetings*." She tried to push past him, but he blocked her way.

"What the devil does that mean?" His tone was surly. "What were you doing?"

A conditioned fury at being grilled flew over her. "Dammit, Tom, I don't have to explain my every move to you!"

Smith paled. He stared at her for a moment, then said, "I'm not Tom. He's dead. I'm Smith. *Smith!*"

"I know that."

"You called me Tom. Dammit, I'm *not* Tom! I won't ever be Tom. And I've been pacing the floor, worried sick about you. I was afraid you'd had an accident or been mugged or kidnapped or—hell, I don't know—something worse." He stormed from the house and slammed the door behind him.

A sick feeling in her stomach rolled over Jessica. Dear God, had she really called him Tom? She hadn't meant to, of course. Maybe it had slipped out because of the familiarity of the argument. Even before his accident, Tom had become almost paranoid about her activities. Afterward, he'd grown worse. Having to account for every movement she made had nearly driven her insane. She couldn't, *wouldn't* go through that again. No way.

That's it. I'm out of here.

Thirteen

Smith strode down a row of grapefruit trees trying to burn off the adrenaline pumping through his body. He wasn't angry, hadn't been angry. He'd been scared, trembling-in-his-boots kind of scared. He was still trembling, but now he had something else to plague him. His worst fears had come to pass when Jessica called him Tom. He'd been right. Despite everything she said to the contrary, she did have them mixed up in her mind. Her Freudian slip had proved that.

He felt as if he'd been poleaxed.

Alternately cursing and praying, he walked the groves in a cold sweat. Finally, he sat down in the dirt and buried his head in his hands. What in the hell was he going to do? He was crazy in love with a woman who was crazy in love with a dead man. His brother. His pitiable, dead twin.

He'd tried to stay away from her, tried with everything that was in him, but she was a fever in his blood, an obsession in his brain. Still, guilt over his feelings for Tom's wife gnawed at him constantly. All of it was tearing him apart. Maybe it would be better if she didn't come back after the Dallas trip. Maybe, in time—

He heard an engine roar to life, and his head came up.

Jess. "Oh, God, no!"

He jumped up and started to run.

Only barely did he make it to the driveway before the RV rounded the side of the house, coming from the barn. He planted himself in its path and waved his arms.

She honked the horn, but he didn't budge. If she left, she'd have to run over him to do it. If he had to fight a ghost for her, he'd do that, too.

The RV stopped, and she sat down on the horn. He stood his ground.

"Get out of the way!" she yelled out the window.

"I'm not moving until we talk!"

"Talk? *Talk?*" she shrieked. "I've been trying to talk to you for days. You've had *meetings!* Move!" She honked again.

"You'll either have to talk with me or run me down. I'm not moving."

There was a long silence. "Okay. Come on in."

He wasn't falling for that one. "Cut the engine first and open the door."

There was another long silence.

Then the engine died, and the door creaked open. That old RV was a piece of crap. He didn't want her driving it in any case.

Before she had a chance to crank up again, he sprinted to the door and climbed in. "Darlin'," he said, taking her hand and motioning to the rear of the RV, "come back here and let's sit down and talk this thing out face-to-face."

Jerking her hand away, she said, "No way. Don't *darlin'* me, and I'm not getting near a bed with you. If you want to talk, sit down in the passenger's seat, and we'll talk."

He sat down.

"So talk," she said, crossing her arms and glaring at him.

"Honey, I'm sorry that I upset you, but I love you, and I was worried sick about you."

"Say that again."

"I was worried sick about you."

"Not that, the other part."

"I'm sorry I upset you."

"No," she said. "The middle part."

"I love you."

"You've never told me that before."

"Sure I have."

She shook her head. "Nope. I've told you a dozen times. You never have. I'd begun to think that I was only a casual affair for you, and you wanted to get rid of me."

"Get rid of you? Oh, God, Jess. I'm crazy about

you, but I start thinking about Tom, and about how you have us all mixed up in your mind, and—"

"Hey! Hold it right there. That's one of the things that we need to discuss. Smith, I don't have you and Tom mixed up in any way. Or at least I didn't until the past few days. I'm sorry that I slipped and called you Tom. I wouldn't have, but the grilling you were giving me sounded just like him. He used to make my life miserable with his jealous, paranoid interrogations. There are things you need to know about Tom and me."

"Honey, I don't need to hear—"

"Oh yes you do. You think that I was madly in love with Tom, and that, in some sick way, I see him reborn in you. Not so. I fell out of love with Tom a long time before he died, a long time before his accident. I suppose I didn't want to disillusion you with the whole ugly story when it served no purpose, but you should know the truth about Tom. He was an alcoholic, surly, withdrawn and impossible to live with. I begged him to go to AA or to a counselor. He wouldn't. I went instead. Counseling saved my sanity and gave me the courage to leave him. We had been separated for several months, and I had filed for divorce two weeks before he got drunk with his buddies and had the accident. I only dropped the suit and went back to Tom because he had no one else to take care of him, and because he desperately needed my insurance coverage."

Sudden fury flashed through him. "Did Tom abuse you?"

"Physically? No. Emotionally? Yes. Almost from

the beginning there were problems. There was a blackness inside Tom, and he refused help. He refused to discuss anything with me. He withdrew, denied and avoided—just the way you've been doing for the past several days. I went through hell, and I won't do it again, Smith. It's best that I leave now. I appreciate all that you've done for me—and for Tom. I'm sorry that you never got to know each other. Maybe you could have helped him. I couldn't.''

"Poor bastard. He didn't have much of a chance, did he?''

"That's not true. He had a tough beginning, and it scarred him, no question of that, but others have had rocky pasts and overcome it. He chose to remain a victim. I came to grips with that a long time ago, and I let him go. Don't make a martyr of him, Smith. And don't be like him.''

"I don't drink.''

"A wise decision for you, I'm sure, given the family history, but that's not what I'm talking about. Don't brood alone and cut yourself off from the people who love you.''

"Do you love me, Jess?'' He took her hand between his.

"Of course I do. But I'm not willing to endure another relationship like the one I had with Tom. Couples need to communicate.''

"Aren't we communicating now?''

She gave a hollow laugh. "I'm doing most of the talking.''

"Let me explain why I've been acting like I

have." He poured out his soul to her, telling her about the guilt he felt for loving her, wanting her, about his fears that he was only a substitute for Tom with her. He told her everything. "Jess, I love you with all my heart. Stay with me and let me prove how much I love you. I swear to God that I'll never grill you again about anything. I may worry, but I'll keep my mouth shut. And I'll do my best to communicate with you about things. I promise." He kissed the palm of her hand and laid it against his cheek. "Give me another chance. Help me do it right."

"If I agree, will you do something for me?"

"Anything. Name it."

"Will you go to Dallas with me and talk to your parents?"

He didn't hesitate. "If that's what you want. Jess, I'd walk through fire for you."

She laughed and stroked his cheek. "I don't need a fire walker. I just want you to be happy. I know that your family loves you and misses you. It's time to talk about the past and put it to rest."

"I've tried. They won't talk."

"I think that this time they will." She fired up the RV.

"Where are you going?"

"Back to the barn."

He grinned. "Ever made love in an RV?"

"Ask me that tomorrow."

Jessica awoke snuggled in Smith's arms and clutching her monkey. She wiggled and stretched.

"Good morning, darlin'," he said, kissing her forehead.

"Good morning."

"Ever make love in an RV?"

She laughed. "Numerous times. How long have you been awake?"

"A while. I've just been watching you sleep. I have to tell you that that's the ugliest monkey I've ever seen in my life."

She covered the monkey's ears. "Don't let Tattoo hear you say that. You'll hurt his feelings. He's my little buddy. Shirley gave him to me as a birthday gift just before I hit the road selling our handbags. She said I needed a sidekick. What time is it?"

He glanced at his watch. "Almost eight. Want some breakfast?"

"Sure. Do you have meetings today?"

He cleared his throat. "Uh…darlin', I have a confession to make."

"A confession?"

"Yes. Promise you won't get mad?"

"I promise nothing. Spill it."

"I haven't had any meetings, that is, not more than a couple that lasted less than an hour."

"Then what have you been doing the last three days?"

"Killing time. Fishing, playing cards, working out at the gym. Doing anything I could to keep my mind off you. It didn't work. You were all I thought about." He brushed his cheek over her forehead. "But all I can think about now is a big stack of pancakes dripping with butter and syrup."

"Gee, thanks." She elbowed him playfully. "Come up. Let's go feed you before you starve."

They dressed and climbed out of the RV.

"Remind me to get a bigger bed for this thing before we try it again," Smith said. "I've got a crick in my neck."

"I'll give you a massage later. I'm a pretty good masseuse. I took lessons when Tom—" She stopped, hesitating to bring up his name. "Sorry."

"Honey, don't be sorry. Your life with Tom is a fact. We can't be tiptoeing around his existence. I'm okay with that now. Is your wrist up to doing neck rubs?"

"Sure is. In fact, the physical therapist dismissed me yesterday. She said I was doing great but to continue home exercises for another few weeks."

"Then book me for a massage, darlin'. Why don't you go shower, and I'll let Rosa know about breakfast. Are pancakes okay with you?"

"Sounds great."

And they were. Although Smith outate her by three to one—actually six pancakes to her two—they both made absolute pigs of themselves.

"I'm going to have to go on a diet," Jessica said. "My jeans are getting hard to zip. Nothing but a salad for me for lunch. And I need to get some exercise. Maybe I'll take up jogging."

"Walking would be better. At least at first. And you'll need a decent pair of shoes before you start. We'll go shopping this morning."

"I can wear my sneakers."

"No," he said emphatically, "you can't. Listen to

your trainer, darlin'. We'll get you the right kind of sport shoes.''

"Yes, coach.'' She smiled, waited until he poured them another cup of coffee, then said, "Have you reconsidered going to Dallas with me? The show starts on Monday. You could talk to your parents while I'm busy with the booth.''

He was quiet for a minute. "Would you go with me to talk to them? We can fly up Sunday. Or maybe we can go Saturday and drive out to Grandpa Pete's. I'd like for you to meet him.''

"Excuse me,'' Rosa said. "There is a telephone call for you, Miss Jessica. Mrs. Myers from Neiman Marcus. You want to call her back?''

"No, no. I'll talk to her now. Thank you, Rosa.''

She took the portable phone Rosa held and turned it on. "Good morning, Sandi. This is Jessica. I just shipped the last of your order yesterday. They should be there tomorrow.''

"I know our customers will be happy to hear that,'' Sandi said, "but I'm calling for a different reason.'' As the buyer talked, Jessica grew more and more excited. Though she maintained her best business manners, she was practically dancing by the time she said, in a super-cool voice, "Sounds like an interesting proposition, Sandi. Let me speak with my partner, and I'll get back to you later today.'' She said her goodbyes, clicked off the phone, then yelled, "Waaaa-hoooo!''

Smith's eyebrows shot up. "Good news I presume?'' He grinned.

"I'll say. Or maybe it's not. Let me think. I'll have

to talk to Shirley, and she's in class. Oh, well, I can get a message to her, and she can call me at her off period or at lunchtime. I can't believe this. I simply can't believe it.''

"Are you going to let me in on the interesting proposition?"

She laughed. "Sorry. I'm rattled. Sandi said that the response to our evening bags has been phenomenal from *all* the stores. They're already sold out again and have a waiting list. They want us to sign an exclusive contract for two years, and they definitely want to showcase our bags in their Christmas catalog! Can you believe it?" She threw herself into his lap and gave him a big kiss.

"What do you think?" she asked.

"I think I'd like another kiss like that one."

"No, no. I mean about the contract. Do you think it's a good idea?"

"It might be. First, you have to decide if you want to sell your bags in only one market. Do you want to keep your operation small and exclusive, or do you want a broader distribution? How many employees will you need for either contingency? How much space? Is that a consideration in your decision? Will they guarantee a minimum order for the contract period? What about the customer base you've already established? Are they excluded in the deal? Is that a problem? In any case, you'll need to have an attorney look over the contract before you sign it."

She kissed him again. "You're a handy guy to have around. I hadn't thought about all those things.

Let's make a list of all the areas we need to consider before I call Shirley.''

"Before or after we go shopping for shoes?"

"I don't have time to shop today. I can do sit-ups. Or maybe I can pump iron in that secret gym you have."

"Secret? It's no secret, darlin'. You're welcome to use it or the pool. Let's go into my study and let Rosa and Ric clean up the table."

They spent an hour going over all angles of Sandi's proposal, then Jessica called Shirley. At noon, Shirley returned her call, and they discussed the matter thoroughly while Smith went for a swim. Jessica telephoned Sandi afterward.

When she hung up, Jessica braided her hair, put on her hot-pink bikini, grabbed the matching jacket and tossed it over her shoulder. There was a definite spring in her step when she went outside.

Tossing the jacket onto a patio chair, she strode to the edge of the pool and dived in. She surfaced beside Smith.

"Hello. What's this?" he asked. "A mermaid?"

"Only me. Shirley and I have reached a decision." She locked her arms around his neck. "Due to the contacts I've already made and the growing traffic from our Web site, the back bag is going great guns. We decided that we aren't interested in becoming a megacorporation with all the accompanying headaches. We hadn't planned on getting rich, just doing well. We'd rather keep our evening-bag operation small and exclusive—and manageable. If we keep production low and quality high, our bags will stay in demand and justify the high price. So, for now at least, we're going to go for the contract with Neiman's, provided they agree to our terms and it meets with the approval of an attorney. Know any good attorneys?''

He grinned. "A couple of dozen."

"Good. Sandi is faxing a copy of their standard agreement as we speak. She didn't seem to think our conditions would be a problem."

"Since the trade show is out now, looks like we'll have to cancel the Dallas trip."

"*Au contraire, monsieur.* You're not going to weasel out of this one. Sandi would like us to come to Dallas, meet her boss and sign the contract next week. Shirley's going to take a personal-leave day and meet us there. We can still talk to your folks. Pick a day.''

Fourteen

──────

"Nervous?" Jessica asked as they drove down the familiar street in Highland Park. Sunday afternoon was quiet in the affluent Dallas area.

"As Grandpa Pete would say, I'm as twitchy as a whore in church. I'm not sure how my folks are going to react to what I'm going to show them. I only told them I was dropping by for a visit with someone I wanted them to meet."

She touched his arm. "It's going to be okay, Smith. You'll see."

"God, I hope so."

When they pulled into the circular driveway of the big brick house, his throat tightened as boyhood memories flooded him.

"Is this where you grew up?" Jessica asked.

He nodded. "It's a lot different from the little shotgun house where Tom lived."

"It's a beautiful home, Smith. There's no reason to feel guilty about a luxurious home. You should feel proud."

"I do now. I never thought about it much growing up. It was just home, and most of my friends lived in the neighborhood. Kyle and I built a tree house in the backyard, just like thousands of other kids." He smiled, remembering. "And my mother worried constantly that we were going to break our necks."

"Like mothers everywhere."

He took a deep breath, then got out of the car. He retrieved his briefcase from the back seat, and he and Jessica walked to the front door.

He rang the bell, and almost immediately the big door swung open.

His mother stood there, her face radiant.

"Smith," she cried, holding open her arms.

"Hello, Mom." He hugged her and spotted his dad standing behind her, smiling broadly as well.

"Son," his dad said, holding out his hand. But when Smith gripped it, his father pulled him into a hug as well, slapping his back. "It's good to have you home."

"Oh, dear," his mother said to Jessica. "Forgive our manners. We're just so happy to see Smith that everything else flew from our heads."

"Mom, Dad," Smith said, pulling Jessica beside him and wrapping his arm around her shoulders. "This is Jessica, a very special lady in my life."

"Mrs. Rutledge, Dr. Rutledge," Jessica said,

greeting them both warmly. They beamed back at her.

Sarah took Jessica's hands. "We're delighted to meet you, Jessica, and so glad you came. Just call us Sarah and T.J. We're not very formal around here, especially since T.J. retired. Come, let's not stand in the foyer. Let's go into the den. I do wish Kyle and Irish could be here, but the baby is only ten days old, and it's nap time for him. They asked if you would stop by later and meet Joshua. He's absolutely precious."

Jessica smiled. "Sounds like you enjoy being grandparents."

"Oh, we do. We can't wait to spoil him."

"Your mother made coffee," his father said to Smith, "and some of that chocolate cake you always liked."

"The one with pecans, Mom?"

"The very one. I'll go cut it."

"Not just yet," Smith said. "Let's go into the dining room. I have some things to show you first."

His mother looked puzzled, his father seemed wary, but they led the way to the dining room where a long mahogany table dominated the space. Smith laid his briefcase on the table, opened it and took out a blown-up copy of the photograph of Tom and Jessica. He placed it on the table, then began to take out other documents and spread them out.

Sarah picked up the picture. "Oh, this is of you and Jessica, but you look so young. It must have been taken ages ago. I didn't realize that—"

"That's not me in the photograph, Mom. That's

Tom Smith, Jessica's former husband. He died two years ago.''

Sarah paled and grabbed for T.J., who eased her into a chair, then took the picture and stared at it. When he glanced up, his expression was grim. "What is this?"

"It's time for the truth, Dad." Smith pointed to the other documents. "This is Tom's birth certificate, and this is mine. These are copies of family medical information, including blood type. This is mine. I don't match anybody in the family. I've researched it all carefully. Last week I received DNA test results that indicate I'm definitely related to a woman named Lula Smith, who's in a nursing home in Oklahoma. She was Tom's grandmother.''

He stared at his mother. "And mine, too, I believe. It's clear that I was adopted. Tom Smith was my twin brother, wasn't he?"

Sarah burst into tears and laid her head on the table. T.J. sat down beside her, comforting his wife, offering her his handkerchief.

"Was this necessary?" his father said. "Look how you've upset your mother."

"Yes," said Smith. "It's necessary. I love you both dearly, but I need to hear the truth from you." He sat down next to his mother and rubbed her back. "Tell me, Mom. It's time."

Her eyes red with weeping, she sat up and looked at him. She stroked his cheek, and love for him shone from her face. "I swore, my dear son. I swore on a Bible that I would never tell you. She wouldn't let us have you otherwise. And you were so tiny and so

sick. If she hadn't left you with us, you would have
died. So I swore." She grasped T.J.'s hand. "We
both swore." She began to cry again.

"Swore what? To whom?"

"Let me tell you the story," his father said. "I
was doing my residency in St. Louis. Kyle was about
two, and your mother was pregnant. In her eighth
month, she had complications. Our baby was stillborn, and Sarah had to have a hysterectomy. She was
still in the hospital, recovering from surgery and ter-
ribly depressed over our loss. At that same time, a
young woman gave birth to twins, and she was in
the room next to your mother."

"Is this the young woman?" Smith pulled the
teenage picture of his birth mother from his briefcase.
"Ruth Smith?"

His father studied the photo. "Yes. This is the one.
Ruth was unmarried and a charity case, part of a
group of flower-children types just passing through
St. Louis, when she went into labor. One boy was
healthy, the other—you—had a heart defect. Our
heart team explained that you would require long-
term, expensive and specialized treatment. Knowing
that she couldn't provide for your needs, she finally
agreed to give you up for private adoption to your
mother and me."

"It was very difficult for her to give you up,"
Sarah said. "Ruth wanted you desperately, but she
knew that she had to think of your welfare. T.J.'s
being a doctor was the deciding factor. She knew that
we could get the very best care for you. Still, giving
you up broke her heart, and she didn't want you to

know that she'd let you go. She made us swear to
two things. That we would never tell you that you
were adopted, and that we would name you Smith.
Her last name was Smith, and she wanted you to
have that legacy from her. We wanted you so desperately that we swore—on a Bible as she insisted."
She stroked his cheek again. "I've wanted to tell you
the truth so many times, but I took that oath seriously. God forgive me for breaking it now."

"Why didn't you take my twin?" Smith asked.

"We wanted to, son," his father said. "We
begged her to let us have you both. I even offered
her a good deal of money. She wouldn't take it. Four
days after you were born, she signed the adoption
papers and left with the other baby and her friends.
She had refused to tell us anything about her background or her family. We never heard from her
again."

"She didn't say who our birth father might have
been?"

"Not a word. Swore she didn't know—though I
suspected that she did. I had planned to question her
again about her family, but she left before I could.
She gave us no clue even as to where she was from."

Smith heaved a big sigh. He felt as if a huge
weight had been lifted from his chest. "So that's it
then? The whole truth."

"The whole truth," his father said. "A colleague
filled out your birth certificate, and you became our
son. Just as Kyle was our son. We moved to Dallas
after my residency was completed the following
year."

Smith stood and pulled his mother to her feet. He hugged her and said, "Mom, I love you. I couldn't have picked a better mother."

She began to cry again. "Oh, look at me. I'm such a blubber-puss. But I love you so much, Smith. Not seeing you or hearing from you nearly broke my heart."

"I promise you'll see a lot of me from now on." Smith hugged his dad as well. "Now, where's that cake?"

His mother laughed and wiped her eyes. "I'll go cut it."

"I'll help," Jessica said. "You know, I love the wallpaper you have in here. We once had a similar pattern in our dining room, except that it was green instead of blue."

The women left, chattering about colors and wallpaper. He could have kissed Jessica for handling his mother so well. He gathered all the evidence spread across the table and returned it to his briefcase.

"How did you locate Jessica?" his father asked.

Smith chuckled. "I didn't locate her. Fate put her in my path, and I thank my lucky stars for that day. She's a wonderful person, and I'm crazy in love with her. We'll tell you and Mom the strange story of how we met—after we have some of that cake." He laughed and slapped his father on the back. "It's good to be home, Dad."

"It's good to have you home, son. Are you two going to get married?"

"I haven't asked her yet, but I plan to soon. You

have her to thank for my coming back. I was too stubborn to do this on my own.''

"Then she's already high on my list.'' His dad threw an arm around Smith's shoulders. ''I can't tell you how much we've missed you.''

They had spent most of the afternoon with Smith's parents, then dropped by to see his brother and meet Joshua, the new baby. Jessica liked Kyle and his wife, Irish, immediately, and Smith got a kick out of seeing his new nephew. Smith and Kyle disappeared into another part of the house for a while, and when they returned, Kyle's arm was draped over Smith's shoulders. Jessica knew that Smith had told his brother about his being adopted, and she could see the peacefulness in Smith's expression.

They had visited for an hour or so, but begged off staying for dinner. Promising to return soon, they left and went back to their hotel for a quiet evening.

"Man, I feel wrung out,'' Smith said that night as they lay in bed.

"But good.''

"But very good.'' He kissed her. ''Thank you.''

"For what?''

"For making me come. And for giving me back my family. I told Kyle this afternoon.''

"I figured that's what you were doing when you disappeared. Was he shocked?''

"He was surprised, but it didn't seem to bother him. We're still brothers. Nothing has changed that. Mom said that she was going to tell Aunt Anna and

Grandpa Pete. Kyle said that he'd take care of telling our cousins."

"It won't change anything with them either."

He kissed her nose, then her eyelids. "You're something else, you know that?"

The following morning, they made the two-hour drive to see Grandpa Pete.

Jessica burst into delighted laughter when she saw the pair of garishly colored stucco tepees. "Are those really rooms?"

"Yep. They're a holdover from the old tourist court days." He pointed to the large weathered log building. "That's his trading post, and he lives upstairs." Pulling the rental car to a stop, he got out and showed her several large wooden sculptures of Indian chiefs, bow-legged cowboys, bears and eagles. "Grandpa Pete carves these with a chain saw."

"A chain saw?" she asked, incredulous. "I can't believe it."

"Believe it. Kyle can do it, too. I never could get the hang of it. Neither could Jackson or Matt. Come on." Taking her elbow, he hurried up the steps to the long gallery that stretched across the front and threw open the door.

"Grandpa Pete!" he shouted. "Where are you, you old coot?"

"No need to holler, boy. Where are your manners?"

An old man stepped out of the shadows. He wore his gray hair in long braids, and his face, wrinkled to show every one of his eighty-something years, was alight with animation. "And who is this beautiful woman on your arm?"

"This is Jessica O'Connor Smith, Grandpa Pete, the light of my life."

Jessica smiled and held out her hand. "I'm happy to meet you, sir. I've heard a lot about you."

"Forget that 'sir' business. Just call me Cherokee Pete—or Grandpa Pete if you're fixing to become part of the family. I like the looks of you, and I've already heard a bit from my daughter. She thinks you're a keeper. You know, Smith here is the last of my grandsons to find a wife. And I won't pussyfoot around about it. Tell you what, Jessica O'Connor Smith, if you'll take him off my hands, I'll give you ten million dollars on your wedding day."

She laughed. "You must be anxious to get rid of him."

He cackled. "Might say that."

"He's serious," Smith said. "How about it? Need ten million?"

She could only stare at him, agape.

Smith winked at her. "We'll discuss this later. Grandpa Pete, I promised Jessica that you'd show her your rattlesnake."

"Sure thing. Right this way, missy. Watch for that bushel of onions. First one I had died. This is a new one Sam Hawkins caught out by his chicken house. It's a jim-dandy. Fourteen rattles, far as I can count. And I'll show you my arrowhead collection. Found every one of them myself—those I didn't get from my grandpa."

Jessica adored Cherokee Pete. Even when he fed

her chili for lunch that seared the skin off the roof of her mouth. She hated to leave that afternoon, but they were meeting Shirley and Mack's flight in Dallas at six, so they had to say goodbye to the old man.

"He's quite a character," she said to Smith as they drove away.

"Nobody else like him. That old man has always been very special to me."

They made it to the airport with time to spare and picked up Shirley and Mack. After checking them in at the hotel, they all changed and went out to dinner, with Smith treating them to a five-star restaurant. He even ordered champagne for the occasion, and he and Jessica joined in with a sip, toasting the success of Jessica Miles Handbags.

"We've come further than I ever imagined," Jessica said. "I can't believe that we'll actually be signing a contract with Neiman Marcus tomorrow."

"Me neither," Shirley said. "When I think of all those lunch periods we spent dreaming up the idea, I really wondered if we would ever get it off the ground. But, by golly, we did. And as chief financial officer of our company, I can say that we're a smashing success. Thanks mostly to your hard work, Jessica."

"Mostly to Smith's contacts, you mean," Jessica said.

"The groundwork was already laid when I came along," Smith said. "You and Shirley and Mack deserve the credit." He raised his glass. "To continued success!"

"Hear! Hear!"

Jessica reached into a small shopping bag she'd brought along and drew out two small packages wrapped in gold paper and tied with blue ribbon. She handed a package to Shirley and one to Mack. "This is a small token to help celebrate this special occasion and to thank you for being such good friends. You were always there every time I needed you, and I love you both dearly."

"You shouldn't have," Shirley said, then grinned, "but you know how I love surprises, and my birthday isn't until October."

They both unwrapped the packages hurriedly. Almost simultaneously, they glanced up with open-mouthed amazement when they saw the gleaming gold watches inside.

"Holy cow, Jessica!" Shirley said. "This is—"

Jessica laughed. "Don't get too excited. They're just knockoffs of the real thing, but don't they look genuine? Smith picked them up for me in Mexico the last time he went to Matamoros. Look, I have one, too." She held up her arm. "Aren't they a kick?"

"Thanks," Mack said. "But they look like the genuine article to me. I've always lusted after one of these babies, but they cost thousands. Are you sure—"

"They're knockoffs," Jessica assured him. "Tell them that they're really fakes, Smith."

Smith winked. "They're really fakes."

"You winked. Why did you wink?" Jessica demanded. "Smith Rutledge, are these watches real?"

He laughed. "I'll never tell."

Fifteen

———

Smith rapped on the bathroom door. "Honey, breakfast is here."

"It can't be. I'm not ready. My hair is a wreck." She flung open the door. "I can't do anything with it."

"Want me to help?"

She rolled her eyes. "I need more of a boardroom look, not a bedroom one. Would you pour me a cup of coffee while I finish my hair?"

"But—"

"Honey, please. My iron level is fine. Dr. Vargas said so. Anyhow, I'm too nervous to eat."

He kissed her nose. "How can I refuse someone so adorable?"

"I'm not adorable. I'm having a bad hair day. It's all lumpy."

He took her hand and dropped the box from his pocket into it. "Maybe this will help. I'll get your coffee."

When he returned with the cup, she hadn't budged from the spot. The box was open, and she was staring at the studs.

"Like 'em?" he asked.

"What's not to like? They're magnificent. Tell me they're CZs."

"They're CZs," he said, setting her coffee cup on the counter. "What's a CZ?"

"A fake diamond."

He locked his arms around her waist. "I don't want you to have fakes. You deserve the real thing."

"But they must be a carat each."

"Two. Like them?"

"I adore them, but I can't accept these. I'd be afraid I'd lose one."

"They're insured. Put them on, love. They'll look great on you, and they'll give you confidence for your meeting this morning. Nobody will even notice your lumpy hair."

She laughed and threw her arms around him. "What am I going to do with you, Smith Rutledge?"

"I'd say I'm a keeper." He started to kiss her.

"Don't you dare! You'll ruin my makeup, and we'll be late."

"Then get a move on, woman. The sooner you sign that contract, the sooner I can have my kiss."

He grabbed a bite while Jessica finished dressing. When she appeared, she almost took his breath away. If he lived to be a hundred, he didn't think he would ever grow tired of just looking at her. And the diamond earrings were perfect. He was eager to give her the ring as well, but that could wait until her nervousness about the meeting had passed.

Too, he was a little nervous about that one. What if she turned him down? He didn't like to think about that possibility.

"Ready?"

She took a deep breath. "Ready. Let's collect Shirley and Mack and get this show on the road."

Jessica and Shirley shook hands with all the bigwigs, then made a gracious exit. Once outside the office, they grinned at each other and made subtle thumbs-up gestures. Once they were in the elevator alone, they fell into each others arms laughing.

"Hot damn!" Shirley said. "Can you believe it? Can you believe it? That contract assures our kids a college education. I can stop teaching tomorrow if I want to."

"Are you going to?" Jessica asked.

"Probably not. I love teaching. How about you? Are you going back to the classroom?"

"I doubt it. I really enjoy what I'm doing more. And besides..."

"There's a certain fella to consider."

Jessica flashed her friend a grin. "That, too."

"I take back what I said about him—about you getting Smith mixed up with a perfected Tom. After being around him more, I can see that he and Tom are very different. He's his own man, and we like him a lot. You love him, don't you, Jess?"

She nodded. "I do."

Shirley hugged her. "Then I wish the very best for you."

"Thanks."

The door swooshed open. Smith and Mack were waiting.

"How'd it go?" Smith asked.

"Smooth as a baby's butt," Shirley said. "I wowed them with my financial genius."

"And I dazzled them," she said, cocking her head to show off the earrings.

"Blinded them is more like it," Shirley said. "Who's for lunch?"

"I am," Mack said. "And it's my treat. How about a burger and fries?"

"Sounds good to me," Smith said. "I know a little place not far from here that has the best grilled hamburgers in town. And their onions rings will make you think you've died and gone to heaven."

"I was just joking about the burger and fries," Mack said, grinning. "I can swing something a little more upscale."

"Actually," Jessica said, "a hamburger sounds mouthwatering."

Half an hour later, the two couples sat on red leather stools at the counter of the little dive that Smith had recommended. The burgers were juicy and wonderful, the fries hot and tasty and the onion rings were beyond heavenly.

"I believe that these onion rings are the best I've ever eaten in my life," Mack said.

"Told you," Smith said. "Next time we all get to

Dallas, I'll take you out for the best spaghetti you ever tasted. Say, Mack, you like to fish. Ever done any deep sea fishing?''

''Not much, but I'd like to.''

''When school's out, plan on spending a week at South Padre Island. Bring the kids. I've got a house there, and they'd love the beach. Jessica can teach them how to use a boogie board.''

''A boogie board?'' she said. ''I don't even know what a boogie board is. And I certainly don't know how to use one.''

''You'll have learned by then,'' Smith said. ''A boogie board is a sissy version of a surf board. They're lots of fun. Do you fish, Shirley?''

''I've been known to wet a worm now and then.''

Smith laughed. ''We'll be using bigger bait than worms, but I think you'll enjoy it. Jess has already become a sailor.''

''I love South Padre,'' Jessica said. ''Promise you'll come, guys.''

''We promise.''

''Great! Pass the catsup.''

After the four finished lunch and Jessica and Smith dropped Shirley and Mack off at DFW, they drove back to Love Field in Dallas and took off in Smith's jet for Harlingen.

She was still smiling when they boarded. Though every detail of the contract was handled by their lawyer and the company's before the signing, the actual putting their names on the line for the generous agreement was a heady experience. What had started out as only a wishful thought had become a reality.

"Happy?" Smith asked as they buckled up.

"Very. And proud of our accomplishment."

When they were airborne, Smith said, "Could I have that kiss now?"

"You betcha."

Their lips met in deep-felt wonderment. His mouth was soft, wet and warm. His tongue, a probing prologue to the desire evident in his touch. His hand covered her breast, then rubbed it gently. Her nipple hardened beneath his fingers. Breathless, she pulled away and laid her forehead against his. "I love you so much, Smith."

"And I love you, Jess. More than I can ever express. You've become the center of my life."

She teased his bottom lip with her teeth. "You're a super-fine man, Smith Rutledge. Not only do I love you, but I like you." Her nose rubbed his. "And my friends like you, too—the expensive watches notwithstanding."

"I like them, and I know how supportive they've been to you. That's why the watches were genuine. I hope you didn't mind."

"No, not really. I suppose when you have lots of money that it's all relative." She snuggled in his arms. "Today was wonderful. The whole weekend was wonderful. I like your family."

"Me, too." He nuzzled her ear. "Want to become part of it?"

She sat up. "What are you asking?"

"I'm asking you to marry me. You can take

Grandpa Pete up on his offer and be ten million dollars richer on our wedding day.''

"I don't need ten million dollars.''

"Will you marry me anyway?''

"I'll have to think about it.''

"Darlin', don't make me wait too long. My heart can't take it.''

She laughed and rubbed noses with him again. "I've thought about it. Yes, I'll marry you.''

"Ever made love on an airplane?'' he asked, cocking one eyebrow and giving her a lusty grin.

"Ask me tomorrow.''

Epilogue

The day couldn't have been more perfect. The grapefruit and orange trees were in full blossom, and their fragrance filled the air with sweet perfume. An arbor, decorated with yellow roses and orange blossoms, was set up on the lawn near the groves, and the wedding guests assembled casually in white chairs.

Smith stood under the arbor with the minister and his brother Kyle, waiting for his bride to appear. He couldn't believe that he'd let Jessica talk him into waiting almost a year for their wedding, but she'd told him that she wanted to be very, very sure they were doing the right thing. Too, she wanted the groves to be in bloom.

They'd opted for a simple wedding with only fam-

ily and a few close friends. And the men wore ordinary suits or sports jackets. Grandpa Pete was tick-
led to death that he didn't have to put on one of
"them danged monkey suits."

His mother and father were in the front row, along
with Irish and baby Joshua, who was walking now.
Behind them, his grandfather sat beside Jackson
Crow and his new wife, Olivia. On his other side
was his cousin Matt Crow and his wife, Eve, who
was Irish's sister. Matt, looking very pleased with
himself, held their new daughter. Congresswoman
Ellen Crow and her brood were there as well. All his
family had come to Harlingen. Every blessed,
blessed one of them.

Smith's heart swelled almost to bursting. He didn't
think he could be any happier.

Then the keyboard player from the small band
they'd hired began the traditional wedding march.
The sound of it stirred strange emotions inside him,
and he looked to the veranda.

Shirley came first. She was dressed in a simple
pink dress and carried a spray of bougainvillea.
Smith quickly looked beyond her. There came the
love of his life on the arm of Mel Cutter. In deference
to Mel's arthritis, they walked slowly.

Dressed in a fluttery, pale yellow gown that Juanita had sewn, Jessica carried an armful of orange and
grapefruit blossoms, the branches carefully stripped
of thorns and tied with yellow ribbons.

She was exquisite. And radiant—as every bride
should be.

Love for her almost brought him to his knees.

Soon she was beside him, repeating their vows. He spoke his own in a clear strong voice, but he silently whispered another vow as he slipped the ring on her finger.

I'll take good care of her, Tom.

* * * * *

presents

DYNASTIES:
THE
CONNELLYS

A brand-new miniseries about the Connellys of Chicago,
a wealthy, powerful American family tied by blood to the
royal family of the island kingdom of Altaria.
They're wealthy, powerful and rocked by
scandal, betrayal...and passion!

Look for a whole year of glamorous and
utterly romantic tales in 2002:

January: **TALL, DARK & ROYAL by Leanne Banks**

February: **MATERNALLY YOURS by Kathie DeNosky**

March: **THE SHEIKH TAKES A BRIDE by Caroline Cross**

April: **THE SEAL'S SURRENDER by Maureen Child**

May: **PLAIN JANE & DOCTOR DAD by Kate Little**

June: **AND THE WINNER GETS...MARRIED! by Metsy Hingle**

July: **THE ROYAL & THE RUNAWAY BRIDE by Kathryn Jensen**

August: **HIS E-MAIL ORDER WIFE by Kristi Gold**

September: **THE SECRET BABY BOND by Cindy Gerard**

October: **CINDERELLA'S CONVENIENT HUSBAND**
by Katherine Garbera

November: **EXPECTING...AND IN DANGER by Eileen Wilks**

December: **CHEROKEE MARRIAGE DARE**
by Sheri WhiteFeather

Where love comes alive™

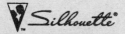

You are invited to enter the exclusive, masculine world of the...

TEXAS Cattleman's Club
The Last Bachelor!

Silhouette Desire's powerful miniseries features five wealthy Texas bachelors—all members of the state's most prestigious club—who set out to uncover a traitor in their midst... and discover their true loves!

THE MILLIONAIRE'S PREGNANT BRIDE
by Dixie Browning
February 2002 (SD #1420)

HER LONE STAR PROTECTOR
by Peggy Moreland
March 2002 (SD #1426)

TALL, DARK...AND FRAMED?
by Cathleen Galitz
April 2002 (SD #1433)

THE PLAYBOY MEETS HIS MATCH
by Sara Orwig
May 2002 (SD #1438)

THE BACHELOR TAKES A WIFE
by Jackie Merritt
June 2002 (SD #1444)

Available at your favorite retail outlet.

Silhouette®
Where love comes alive™